"I was a virgin."

Vic felt dizzy at the realization of what he'd done. He'd taken something from Angela through deception. If he'd known...he never would have come on so strong.

"Why didn't you tell me?" he asked in a hoarse voice.

"I didn't want you to change your mind. Men like you run from virgins. I'm sorry."

"You don't have to apologize for giving me an incredible gift." *He* was the one who should be apologizing. But to do that, he'd have to confess this night started off as a setup....

Dear Reader,

Come join us for another dream-fulfilling month of Harlequin American Romance! We're proud to have this chance to bring you our four special new stories.

In her brand-new miniseries, beloved author Cathy Gillen Thacker will sweep you away to Laramie, Texas, hometown of matchmaking madness for THE LOCKHARTS OF TEXAS. Trouble brews when arch rivals Beau and Dani discover a marriage license—with their names on it! Don't miss *The Bride Said, "I Did?"*!

What better way to turn a bachelor's mind to matrimony than sending him a woman who desperately needs to have a baby? Mindy Neff continues her legendary BACHELORS OF SHOTGUN RIDGE miniseries this month with *The Horseman's Convenient Wife*—watch Eden and Stony discover that love is anything but convenient!

Imagine waking up to see your own wedding announcement in the paper—to someone you hardly know! Melinda has some explaining to do to Ben in Mollie Molay's *The Groom Came C.O.D.*, the first book in our HAPPILY WEDDED AFTER promotion. And in Kara Lennox's *Virgin Promise*, a bad boy is shocked to discover he's seduced a virgin. Will promising to court her from afar convince her he wants more than one night of passion?

Find out this month, only from Harlequin American Romance!

Best wishes,
Melissa Jeglinski
Associate Senior Editor

Virgin Promise

KARA LENNOX

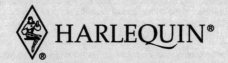 HARLEQUIN®

TORONTO • NEW YORK • LONDON
AMSTERDAM • PARIS • SYDNEY • HAMBURG
STOCKHOLM • ATHENS • TOKYO • MILAN • MADRID
PRAGUE • WARSAW • BUDAPEST • AUCKLAND

For my husband, Rob

ISBN 0-373-16840-3

VIRGIN PROMISE

Copyright © 2000 by Karen Leabo.

This edition published by arrangement with Harlequin Books S.A.

Visit us at www.eHarlequin.com

Printed in U.S.A.

ABOUT THE AUTHOR

Texas native Kara Lennox has been an art director, typesetter, advertising copy writer, textbook editor and reporter. She's worked in a boutique, a health club and has conducted telephone surveys. She's been an antiques dealer and briefly ran a clipping service. But no work has made her happier than writing romance novels.

When Kara isn't writing, she indulges in an ever-changing array of weird hobbies, from rock climbing to crystal digging. But her mind is never far from her stories. Just about anything can send her running to her computer to jot down a new idea for some future novel.

Dear Reader,

I can't imagine any career more satisfying—or more fun—than writing romance novels. After writing dozens of books over the past few years for different romance lines and different publishers, I'm especially happy to have found a home with Harlequin American Romance, a line I've been reading since its launch.

Virgin Promise was a fun story to write, probably because my cautious, organized heroine, Angela, who plans every detail of her life, is nothing like me! I always wondered how such people cope when they fall crazy in love. Here, at least, is one theory about what might happen. Poor Angie doesn't know what hit her, and Vic, the steady, reliable cop she falls in love with, doesn't fare much better! Eventually, of course, they figure it all out. But I tortured them a bit along the way. (Authors get to do that.)

I hope you enjoy *Virgin Promise*, and I look forward to sharing more fun stories with you in the future.

Sincerely,

Kara Lennox

Prologue

"It was in the back seat of my mother's station wagon at the local lovers' lane."

Angela Capria listened to her friend Phoebe's sordid confession with a mixture of discomfort and fascination. Fascination because her friends looked so normal, yet each one shocked her anew with their tales of painful embarrassment. Discomfort, because she'd already heard three humiliating anecdotes during the past half hour. Her turn was rapidly approaching.

She wasn't sure how the subject had come up, but over pasta salad and diet Cokes at their favorite deli, Angela's co-workers had spontaneously started confessing how they'd lost their virginity, sparing no details.

"I was sixteen," Phoebe, a bouncy physical therapist, continued in a hushed voice, "and he was the biggest nerd in the entire school. But he was crazy about me, and, you know, when a guy's crazy in love with you, it's really an aphrodisiac."

Angela was appalled. "So, you didn't have any

feelings for this guy, but you had sex with him anyway?''

''Well, I felt sorry for him. You know how that goes.''

The other three women nodded their commiseration, much to Angela's confusion. Why would anyone, even a sixteen-year-old, have sex with someone out of pity? Sex was such a...a personal thing. A powerful and special gift that a woman gave to a man after careful consideration. Or at least that was how it worked in Angela's universe. Anyway, she thought so.

''So, how was it?'' someone asked Phoebe.

''Terrible, of course. The guy needed a flashlight and a guide book.''

Everyone laughed, including Angela. Phoebe had a way with words. As the laughter faded, however, Angela realized four pairs of curious eyes were riveted on her. She cleared her throat and looked down into her salad, playing with an olive she had no intention of eating.

''Well, Angie?'' Phoebe prompted. ''Your turn.''

''No, thanks,'' Angela said politely.

''Aw, c'mon,'' said Victoria, a refined blond nurse who fifteen minutes ago had admitted she'd been so drunk during her deflowering she didn't even remember it.

''It couldn't be worse than mine.'' The usually shy Sarah, their clinic's office manager, piped up. She was the only one in the group who was married, and she'd turned bright red as she'd confessed that she'd been an awkward virgin bride.

"We won't laugh," said redheaded Terri, the clinic's receptionist, who only minutes earlier had sent the whole table into hysterics with her tale of whipped cream and a rubber spatula.

Angela daintily blotted her mouth with her napkin. "All right. You asked for it. But I think you'll be shocked."

"I'm a nurse," Victoria said. "You can't shock me."

Angela took a deep breath. "I've never had sex with anybody. I'm still a virgin."

Phoebe dropped her fork. It rolled across the floor with a cherry tomato still attached, but no one bent to retrieve it. They all just stared, mouths gaping.

"Angie, honey, that's impossible," Phoebe said, breaking the uncomfortable silence. "You're twenty-six years old!"

"And you're so…so…" Sarah couldn't find the word.

"Earthy, I think is what she's trying to say," Terri put in. "Sensual. I mean, you're a massage therapist, for gosh sake."

Angela waited for their objections to die down and the inevitable question to arise. "Why?" they asked, almost as one.

"'Cause I've never met a guy who made me so crazy with lust or desire or pity or whatever that I was willing to risk pregnancy, disease, or the emotional vulnerability that goes with sex. There, I've said it.''

Terri sighed. ''You mean you've never felt carried away by the moment? Like where you just don't give a flip about the consequences of your actions?''

Angela shook her head. ''Never.'' She took a small bite of her brownie, savoring the rich chocolate indulgence and hoping the subject would drop. No such luck.

''So, like, do you think it'll ever happen?'' Phoebe asked cautiously. ''I mean, you do *like* guys, right?''

Oh, honestly. Did they think she was frigid? ''Yes, of course I like guys, and of course it'll happen. When I meet the right man, and I have a long-term, secure relationship, that's when I'll be ready to take the appropriate steps.''

''Honey, it's not line dancing,'' Phoebe said with a wink. ''And believe me, if you sit around waiting for 'the right guy,' you'll be a virgin when you're eighty. Just what qualities, exactly, does this mythical paragon of yours possess?''

Angela gave the question serious consideration. ''He would have to be psychologically mature. Responsible and reliable. Stable, with the kind of job I can respect. A hard worker. Open and, most important, completely honest.''

''Bo-o-o-oring,'' the others said in unison.

Phoebe got a thoughtful look on her face. ''I'll bet,'' she said slowly, waiting until she had everyone's attention, ''I'll bet that's your problem. You've been looking for all the wrong things. If the right guy came along—tall and dark, dangerous and mysterious—and he pushed all the right buttons, you'd be putty in his hands.''

The others nodded in agreement.

Angela shrugged. ''Maybe so.'' She almost wished it were true. She *was* a passionate, sensual person. Deep down, she knew that. She reveled in all of her senses, but particularly touch. That was why she was such a good massage therapist. Still, she'd never experienced that all-consuming lust her friends raved about. Maybe it was just bad luck. Maybe the right guy hadn't come along.

And maybe she wouldn't have any idea what to do if he did. It was a sobering thought.

Chapter One

Angela cursed three times, stamped her foot and beat on the windshield glass with her fist, but her temper tantrum did nothing to change the situation. First her car had refused to start. Then, when she'd stomped off to find a phone to call her motor club, she'd locked her keys inside the car. She was out here in the clinic parking lot at a quarter past nine in the evening, and everything she owned was locked inside, including her purse. She didn't even have thirty-five cents on her to make a call from a pay phone. All she had going for her was that things couldn't get worse.

As the full wretchedness of her situation dawned on her, she became aware of a rumbling that grew louder. Whirling around, she saw a man on an awesomely big motorcycle slowly approaching. Suddenly her situation seemed a whole lot worse than it had just seconds ago.

She should run, she thought, though her feet remained stubbornly planted to the asphalt. Her eyes were riveted on the broad shoulders of the biker, the way his faded denim shirt stretched across his chest.

His powerful thighs, covered by yet more denim, gripped the bike, and his black-leather-gloved hands held the handlebars in what looked like a gentle caress.

A tinted visor across the front of his helmet hid his face, but Angela knew he was looking at her. Staring, in fact.

Though a stranger in a dark parking lot represented unspeakable danger, Angela was fascinated. She couldn't turn her gaze away, much less run. A tightness claimed her chest and a slight queasiness assaulted her stomach. The feeling reminded her of riding the Ferris wheel at the State Fair—exhilarating, but scary.

The bike pulled up beside her. The rider pulled off his helmet, revealing a full head of thick, black, wavy hair, a bit shorter than she'd expected. He smoothed it off his forehead in a fluid gesture, all the while staring at her.

Then she saw his eyes. They were a piercing blue, so vivid she could easily detect the color even in this dimly lit scenario. They almost glowed, as if they had a light of their own. They were topped with steeply angled, dramatic eyebrows and rimmed with thick lashes. His long nose might have been aquiline once, but it looked as if it had been broken a few times. His cheekbones were razor sharp, his lips full and sensual, his chin square as a brick and just as stubborn looking.

She took in all of his features instantaneously,

though for a moment it seemed time stood still as they stared at each other.

"Problem?" he asked in a deep, almost gravelly voice. A whiskey voice. She'd read that in a book once, but only now understood the meaning of the phrase.

Somehow she found her own voice. It even managed to come out sounding fairly normal. "It won't start. Then I locked my keys inside."

"Double trouble," he said, turning off the bike. He swung one leg behind him and dismounted. His innate animal grace made Angela's mouth go dry. In two strides he was very close, and for one agonizing moment she thought he was going to grab her. Instead he stepped around her, leaned down and peered into the driver's window.

"Yeah, there they are, all right."

"You didn't believe me?"

"I like to see things for myself. What's your name?"

"Angela," she blurted out. God, what was wrong with her? She shouldn't give out her name to a perfect stranger.

"Angela," he repeated. Her name coming out of his mouth had an erotic turn to it she'd never heard before. "Well, Angela, got a coat hanger?"

She noticed he didn't offer his own name in return. "No. Actually, I think I'll just go find a phone and call someone…" As she spoke, she edged away from him, overwhelmed by the overt maleness of him. He wasn't huge—she'd give him six foot one—but there was something about him, a barely leashed power, a dangerous essence, that made her uneasy even as it fascinated her.

"Hold on, now. Maybe I can help you out." He sidled past her and went to the trunk, popping it open with one deft movement. "You don't lock your trunk?"

"There's nothing in there anyone would want to steal."

"Just a spare tire and a jack. And—" he grabbed something from her trunk and held it aloft triumphantly "—a coat hanger." He slammed the trunk shut and immediately began untwisting the wire hanger. Angela watched, utterly enthralled, as he manipulated the pliant metal into a curved hook. He'd obviously done this a time or two, which only added to her uneasiness.

"Maybe I should just go call the auto club," she ventured, knowing now she'd made a mistake. She never should have let this frightening stranger take control of the situation away from her. Hadn't she learned anything in her assertiveness-training class?

"They'll take forever to get here," the stranger argued as he returned his attention to the locked door, then felt expertly along the edge of the window for just the right point of entry. "It's St. Patrick's day. Drunks all over Dallas are running out of gas, flattening their tires on broken beer bottles and losing their keys. Trust me, you don't want to be out here alone."

He had a point. Angela stood back a few feet, ready to flee at the slightest provocation. But the stranger, frightening as he was, hadn't made any threatening gestures or comments. Then again, he didn't have to. His mere presence was intimidating enough.

He made several tries at the lock, then pulled the hanger out and reshaped it slightly.

"You've done this before," she said.

"Yeah." He inserted the hanger again. "Hell, there's not a car made I can't get into."

Oh, that was comforting.

"Comes from a misspent youth. Hah!" He gave the coat hanger one final yank, and the door lock gave. In seconds he had the front door open.

She was so relieved, so anxious to retrieve her precious keys, that she forgot to be cautious. She slid right past him, only belatedly realizing her body would brush against his. She received a brief impression of heat and hardness before she gained the relative safety of the driver's seat. His physical allure was undeniable.

She refused to look at him, afraid of what she would see in those luminescent blue eyes. Mostly she was afraid she would see acknowledgment of what *she* felt—awareness. Awareness on a totally physical, sexual level.

It was a preposterous thing for her to admit, but it was true. She'd felt desire before. She'd even been tempted, at least mildly, to break the celibacy habit. But for her, physical awareness had always followed emotional closeness. She'd never just looked at a guy, heard his voice, watched his hands and felt a rush of heat wash through her like liquid fire.

All wrapped up in this crazy flush of lust was her fear. She was completely vulnerable to him. He was big and undoubtedly strong, and he could have her under his control in a heartbeat. Her smartest course of action, she knew, was to get the hell out of there. Grab her purse and her keys, lock up her car and flee.

"Thanks so much for helping me out," she said in an attempt to end the encounter. "I don't know what I would have done…"

He wasn't listening to her. He leaned through the open car door, and for one glorious, hideous moment she thought he was going to kiss her. Then he sank lower, leaning in farther, and her engine hood popped open. He'd been searching for the release lever.

"Really, you don't have to—"

"It's no trouble," he said, withdrawing, but not before Angela got a noseful of his scent—clean, like soap, but with a hint of musk. He probably hadn't showered in the past thirty minutes, but the essence was enough to convince Angela that the man had good grooming habits. That didn't exactly fit the Hell's Angel image given off by the rest of him.

Resigned, Angela climbed out of the car with her purse and car keys firmly in hand—in case she decided to run away after all. But despite his daunting appearance, the man had been nothing but helpful so far, she reasoned. If he'd wanted to do something terrible, he'd probably have done it already.

With that comforting thought in mind, she stood passively by and let the man try to fix her car. She didn't normally allow fate or luck to dictate her behavior, but tonight she felt powerless to divert the freight train of events barreling along the tracks in her personal universe.

She was taking an enormous chance by trusting this man. Yet she didn't seem to have any choice. For the first time in her life, Angela Capria had been swept off her feet.

And the guy wasn't even trying! Imagine the results if he put a little effort into it.

WHAT THE HELL AM I DOING? Vic Steadman thought, as he fiddled pointlessly with the woman's car engine. The distributor cap had been unscrewed, a fully deliberate effort someone had made to disable her vehicle. With a twist of his hand he could have her engine running and send her on her way.

That's why he'd come, right? To make sure the woman wasn't stranded all alone in a dark parking lot? But he didn't fix the car. Instead he checked fluid levels, disconnected and reconnected hoses, checked points and plugs, all in an effort to buy himself some time. What did he really want to do here?

He'd never expected Angela Capria to be so gorgeous.

A few hours ago, when his rookie partner, Bobby Ray Allen, had lain on the gurney getting stitched up in the Parkland E.R. after an unfortunate confrontation with a beer bottle, he'd confessed his problem to Vic. It seemed he had a blind date, and there was no way he was going to make it out of the E.R. in time to meet her. Would Vic pinch-hit for him?

Vic had considered this a very peculiar request. Normally Bobby had plenty of female company and didn't need fix-ups. Also, Bobby was territorial about his girlfriends. He seldom introduced any of the guys on the force to his various women, much less invited one of his buddies to fill in for him on a date. If Bobby hadn't been lying there bleeding, Vic would have suspected he was being set up.

"Why can't you just call her?" Vic had wanted to know.

Then Bobby had explained the unusual circumstances, and Vic had been stuck. Apparently this woman refused blind dates. So her friends had covertly set her up. They'd sabotaged her car, and Bobby was supposed to rescue her, then sweep her off her feet with a dark, dangerous, sexy persona.

If Vic hadn't filled in, the poor woman would have been stranded out here alone in a questionable neighborhood.

He'd originally planned to identify himself as a Dallas cop so as not to scare her, then fix her car and send her on her way. But that was before he'd seen her.

"Do you see the problem?" the woman asked anxiously.

"Not yet," he lied.

From the way Bobby had talked about her, he'd been expecting some homely, sexually repressed spinster. Nothing could be farther from the truth.

Angela was in her mid-twenties, slender, with rich dark hair pulled into a loose braid and shapely curves that not even her sexless nurse's whites could disguise. Her breasts were high and full, more than a handful, and her hips were gently rounded beneath the white slacks. He wasn't sure what color her eyes were, other than that they were dark, but her mouth was incredible—full, moist and pink.

As he thought about that mouth and all the things it might be persuaded to do, Vic felt a stirring inside him, like a sleeping beast opening one eye. Though the foreignness of the feeling concerned him, he couldn't help but smile at the imagery that had come to mind. Him? A beast? He was reliable, steady Steadman.

Incredibly, his police badge never came out of his pocket. Instead, during that split second he had to assess her, he racked his brain for everything Bobby had told him about her. Massage therapist…repressed…needs a fantasy man to sweep her off her feet, someone dark and dangerous to take control out of her hands, to push her buttons, to awaken her sexuality.

Without any conscious decision on his part, he'd found himself becoming that dark, dangerous fantasy man. He'd stopped short of actually frightening her, because that wasn't in him under any circumstances, but he'd definitely taken control away from her.

"Looks like it might be your distributor," he said, hoping she didn't know much about car engines. "I could fix it if I had my tools."

"It's okay," she said. "I don't live far. I'll just call

a friend to pick me up, and deal with the car tomorrow.''

That thought made him uneasy. Any mechanic would immediately spot the sabotage, and she would know Vic had pulled a fast one. He quickly formulated a plan. ''If you don't live far, I'll give you a lift,'' he offered.

The woman's eyebrows shot up. ''On that?'' She nodded toward his cycle.

''Sure, why not?''

He could tell she was intrigued. ''I've never ridden a motorcycle before.''

He shrugged. ''Nothing to it. I do all the driving. You just hold on to me.''

She shook her head. ''I'd have to have a helmet, and I won't take yours.''

He sauntered over to his motorcycle, opened the side compartment and produced an extra helmet. He dangled it by the chin strap, almost like bait. ''Any more objections?''

Angela licked her lips and cocked her head, still indecisive. She would have to be crazy to go with him, he thought. He hadn't even offered her a name. But she felt the same sexual pull he had. He'd seen it on her face, in her eyes, during those first few moments when they'd simply stared at one another.

''Do you promise to go slowly?''

''I haven't had a ticket in years.''

''All—'' Her voice cracked, and she took a moment to clear her throat. ''All right. I appreciate it very much.''

"Pleasure's all mine." He gave her a long look before he climbed aboard the bike. She hesitated another moment, then took the extra helmet and set it on her head. He had to help her adjust the strap. His knuckles brushed against the ivory smoothness of her cheek, sending ribbons of warmth trickling through his body. Damn, if her cheek did this to him, imagine what her other body parts might accomplish.

No, maybe it was better not to think of that. He had no idea how far this would go, but he didn't imagine Angela would invite him into her bed no matter how powerful the fantasy. He didn't believe she was that impulsive.

After donning his own helmet, he extended a hand to her for support. She grabbed it and clambered aboard behind him.

That first touch of her hand to his jolted him to another level of awareness. He'd never been so conscious of the feel of a woman's hand before, the smoothness, the soft pads of her fingers. She wiggled around, settling in, and he nearly jumped out of his skin. He was supposed to be the one in control, yet he was the one whose brain was short-circuiting. He imagined how her cute butt looked wiggling on the black leather seat.

She tucked her purse between their bodies, but there was still plenty of contact as she leaned forward and wrapped her arms around him in a snug, warm embrace.

Vic could have sat there all night, just feeling her soft breasts pressed against his back. He could even smell her, and she smelled like coconut and almonds. As a massage therapist, she probably slathered scented lotions on her hands all day long.

"Where to?" he asked.

"Oh. On Seymour and Huntington, the Huntington Terrace Apartments. Do you know where that is?"

"I'll find it." And if he made a wrong turn by accident, well, a few extra minutes of this exquisite torture wouldn't kill him. Maybe.

With a turn of the ignition key the bike rumbled to life beneath them.

The evening was beautiful, the air warm but still with the crispness of spring. The streets of Angela's Oak Lawn neighborhood were filled with St. Patrick's Day revelers, and he was glad she didn't have to wander around by herself. Normally the eclectic area Dallas called Oak Lawn was pretty safe—he'd once ridden a beat here as a bicycle cop—but muggings and car break-ins weren't unheard of, especially when so much drinking went on.

The roar of the cycle's engine precluded talking, but Vic enjoyed the ride immensely. He was disappointed when he found her apartment building with no trouble.

The building was an old one, probably built in the 1930s, a humble, three-story brown-brick structure with an inviting front porch surrounded by mature trees. Small air-conditioning units protruded out many of the windows, so this wasn't one of those luxurious renovations with sky-high rents. But it looked reasonably well taken care of. The walkway was lined with daffodils, and pots of orange geraniums decorated the front porch.

He pulled into a no-parking zone right in front and cut the engine.

Slowly Angela released her grip around his middle and eased herself away from him. "That wasn't so bad," she said, more to herself than to him.

He was a little surprised to hear her say that. Normally he was a very conscientious rider. Working the traffic division, he'd seen firsthand the devastation that could be done to the human body when it flew off a motorcycle at high speeds. But he'd driven a hair faster than normal tonight—nothing unsafe, but enough to get Angela's adrenaline flowing.

Enough to add to the aura of danger.

She removed her helmet and handed it to him, her hands shaking slightly. "Thanks for everything. I'd have been in quite a mess if you hadn't come along." Her voice was a little bit breathless.

"No charge. I'll see you to your door."

"That's not—"

"I know it's not necessary. What if there's a mugger waiting in the lobby?" He didn't wait for her permission, but climbed off the bike, removed his own helmet and followed her up the steps to the porch. Her hand shook as she stuck the key in the front door lock. She pulled open the door a crack, then turned to face him.

"I'm in," she said. "Thank you. And good night."

He could see, now, that he'd made her uneasy. He hadn't meant to. It was this new, dark and dangerous evil twin inside him that had done it by refusing to let her dismiss him. And it was the evil twin who leaned over and stole a kiss.

He didn't touch her with anything but his lips. She could have backed off at any time, kicked him in the shins, screamed, whatever she wanted. But she just stood there, passively accepting the light pressure of his mouth against her soft, soft lips. Other than a telltale quiver and the flutter of her tentative hand against his chest, she didn't react.

But he did. That dozing beast inside him opened both eyes wide and snorted to life. He felt the tightness in his groin, the pleasurable curls of desire warming his belly.

Suddenly Angela lost her balance. The door closed behind her, and she fell against it, breaking the kiss.

For a moment all she could do was stare at him, her eyes smoky with desire but wary as hell. Did he blame her?

"Please…" she said.

"Please…what?"

"I can't ask you inside."

He ran one forefinger along her jaw. "You could if you wanted," he whispered, amazed at his own bravado. He was acting like one of those guys in the movies he hated, the ones who were so damn sure of their sex appeal that it never entered their minds that a woman might not be willing. He considered himself confident when it came to the opposite sex, but not pushy.

"I don't even know you!"

"But you trust me just the same."

Unwillingly, it seemed, she nodded. On some level she must have sensed that he was one of those serve-and-protect types, not a taker or a defiler of women, despite his cocksureness.

When she made no further move to escape, but just stared at him with an expression he couldn't read, he finally figured it out. She was his for the taking. She couldn't ask him in, because she was a nice girl, and nice girls didn't ask strange men into their apartments. But if he invited himself, she wouldn't turn him away.

He'd accomplished Bobby Ray's mission, and it had been surprisingly easy. She was his, at least for this night.

Somehow, that realization didn't make him feel overjoyed. Yeah, maybe he could sweet-talk his way into her bedroom, and they could spend one awesome night indulging in mindless sex. But that would be the end of it. Instinctively, he knew that.

She deserved better than that. Much as it pained him, he would have to deny himself the pleasures of Angela's body—for a while, anyway.

He cupped her face between his palms and kissed her again, as if he meant it. This time she was anything but passive. She tilted her head and opened her mouth, eagerly accepting the thrust of his tongue. She put her arms around him, drawing his body closer until they were hip to hip, chest to chest.

He wanted more than anything to remove the barrier of clothing between them, to lie beside Angela and feel her warm, smooth flesh all up and down his own body, to explore every inch of her with his hands and mouth. It took all his willpower to pull away.

She looked up at him, questioning, breathing hard.

He brushed one last kiss on her forehead. "I have to go. Good night, Angela."

She swallowed. "Good night, then."

He turned and walked toward his bike without a backward glance, though he ached from his toes to his scalp. Delaying gratification would make it that much better, he told himself, hoping he hadn't messed this thing up royally. What if, by tomorrow, she'd come to her senses and wanted nothing to do with him?

But as long as he remained her dark and dangerous fantasy man, she would be interested. He was counting on that.

"Hey!" Angela called out, startling him. "You never told me your name!"

He waved goodbye, but he didn't answer her.

Chapter Two

Angela walked to work the next morning. She could have called Phoebe or Victoria to give her a lift; both of them lived nearby. But she didn't think she could face either of them just yet. What if they asked her how she'd gotten home last night when her car had broken down?

So she walked. The weather was cool and crisp, and the forty-five-minute "urban hike" helped clear her head.

She had no idea what had gotten into her last night. The moment she'd seen that dangerous-looking man approach, she should have run like a rabbit. She'd learned in a self-defense class that avoiding conflict was a woman's first, best defense. But no, she'd stood there like a deer blinded by headlights.

Getting on the back of his motorcycle had been sheer insanity. She hated motorcycles. They were dangerous. Though she had to admit her mystery man was a good rider—he hadn't lied about that. The large bike gave a surprisingly smooth ride, and once she'd figured out how to lean into the turns and move her body in sync with his, she'd found herself enjoying the trip.

That didn't change the fact that she'd thought nothing of throwing her arms around a complete stranger, pressing herself against his back and inhaling that sexy, soap-and-starch smell of him. She'd almost been sorry when they reached her building.

By the time she climbed off the bike, her senses had been so full of him she could hardly stand up straight. And when he'd leaned down to kiss her, any semblance of control she'd maintained had faded into the warm spring night.

He never should have assumed she would be receptive to his advances just because he'd helped her out of a jam. Yet he had, and damn it, he'd been right. Any sane woman would have slapped him silly. But that reaction wouldn't have made sense in her case, not when she'd been consumed with lust herself.

If he'd been a cad, he'd have taken advantage of the situation and had his wicked way with her.

"Oh, why didn't he?" she asked, not realizing she'd spoken aloud until a woman waiting on the corner with her for the light to change gave her a funny look. The realization that she would have made love to a man after less than an hour's acquaintance rocked her to her foundations. But she couldn't deny the regret weighing down her heart.

She was so flustered she had to concentrate to remember the way to work.

When she reached the clinic it was still early, so she ducked into the doughnut shop across the street and bought a dozen glazed twists for the office. By the time she returned to the clinic, most of the office staff had arrived. Her pastries were greeted with enthusiasm and gratitude, distracting everyone so she could slip into her office.

But her luck didn't hold out. She was just unlocking her office door when she was accosted by Phoebe and Victoria.

"Hey, Angie," Phoebe said. "We were wondering where you were. We saw your car, but you weren't here."

"I ducked into the doughnut shop," she said. "There's a box of glazed twists in the break room." She hoped they'd take the hint, but they followed her right into her office like a couple of puppies.

Phoebe found a perch on the edge of Angela's massage table. "So, anything interesting going on in your life?"

Angie gave an indifferent shrug.

If they only knew! Did it show on her face? she wondered. Did her obsession with the mystery man ooze out of her pores? She studied her fingernails with casual indifference, then pulled out a nail file and went to work. Ragged nails were anathema to a massage therapist.

"When we saw your car," Victoria said, "and the clinic was still locked, we were worried."

Shoot. She might as well fess up, or they were going to pick the truth out of her. She'd never been much good at keeping secrets. "Actually, last night is when you should have been worried. My car didn't start, and you two buzzed out of the lot so fast you didn't even notice.''

In unison, they gasped melodramatically.

''Oh, Angie, honey, we're so sorry!'' Phoebe said. ''What did you do?''

She took a deep breath. Confession was good for the soul, right? ''A Good Samaritan gave me a ride home.''

Phoebe and Victoria exchanged a glance.

''You got into a car with a perfect stranger?'' Victoria asked, sounding more intrigued than disapproving.

''He, um—''

''He?'' Phoebe repeated, arching one suggestive eyebrow.

Angela ignored her. ''He was riding a motorcycle, actually.''

''A motorcycle!'' the two other women squealed together.

''Look, he was very nice, he dropped me off at my door and now I'm calling the motor club.'' She stood and opened the office door, gesturing for her friends to beat it. ''If you please? I have a client scheduled in ten minutes.''

They looked a bit bewildered, but they left. Angela closed the door and sank back into her chair. How could one— Okay, two little kisses completely destroy her composure?

God, those were the best kisses. They'd been not just a turn-on, they'd transformed her, melted her into an abject pool of acquiescence. What was she to do with a man like that? Not that she'd ever get a chance to do anything, she reminded herself. He was gone forever, and she hadn't even gotten his name. He probably liked it that way. No telling how many foolish women he'd have trailing after him if he gave out his name and phone number like so much candy.

Maybe she should have invited him in. At least she would have been taking back some of her normal control. Last night she had felt about as far out of control as she could ever remember.

Wearily she dialed the motor club for a tow to her regular mechanic. When they asked for her license plate number, she couldn't remember it.

"Um, just one second, I'll have to look it up," she said. She put the call on hold, then went to her window, which faced the parking lot. What she saw there took her breath away. The hood of her car was open, and a man was leaning over working on the engine, giving her a fabulous view of his butt. And what a butt.

Though she couldn't see his face, she knew who her mystery mechanic was. Her heart leapt with joy. She was being given a second chance to be foolish, and she was deliriously happy.

She grabbed up the receiver. "Uh, never mind. The problem with my car seems to have taken care of itself." She hung up and ran out of her office, not even bothering to explain to Terri where she was going in such a hurry as she sped past the receptionist's desk.

Angela paused at the exterior door to catch her

breath. What was she going to say? It might pay to be prepared, to have a plan so she wouldn't fly by the seat of her pants like last night.

She would be completely in control this time. *That* was her plan. She wouldn't let him lead her into anything she wasn't ready for.

The question remained, though—what exactly was she ready for?

You've never felt carried away by the moment? Terri's question at lunch the other day haunted Angela. She'd remained a virgin all these years because she'd never been faced with a compelling enough reason to change her status. Was this bad-boy Good Samaritan her compelling reason?

Maybe. But she absolutely was not going to rush into anything. She would get to know him first, find out exactly what sort of person he was.

Squaring her shoulders, she emerged from the building and walked resolutely into the parking lot. She approached the man quietly, because she wanted the element of surprise on her side, but somehow he sensed her sneaking up on him. He straightened and turned, a lazy smile brightening his foreboding features.

"Good morning."

"Hi," she returned. For the first time, she felt a bit irritated with his high-handedness. She hadn't given him permission to work on her car. "How did you get my hood open?"

"I have my ways."

Ye gods. Her stomach fluttered. He looked good

this morning in black jeans and a dark green cotton shirt rolled up at the sleeves. Overlooking that, it was on the tip of her tongue to tell him to cease and desist, that she would take care of her own car, thank you very much.

But he spoke again. "I think I have the problem fixed. Want to give it a try?"

The driver's door was already unlocked. As he closed the hood, she slid behind the wheel and felt around for the spare key she kept under the floor mat. Yes, there it was. She cranked the ignition, and the car started up immediately, the engine humming smoothly. In truth, it sounded a lot better than it had in months.

She shut it off and got out again. "What did you do to it?"

"Fixed the distributor. There were some, er, loose connections. Then I tuned it up. You need an oil change."

"Thanks very much," she said, meaning it. She'd had several unexpected expenses the past couple of months, and she couldn't really afford a big car repair bill. "Can I pay you for your trouble?"

"Consider it a favor between friends."

"We aren't friends," she was quick to point out. "I don't even know your name."

"Vic. Vic Steadman."

Finally. She repeated the name several times in her head, trying to decide if it suited him. It was a sturdy-sounding name. What had she been expecting, something scary? Blade Black, maybe, or Dirk Danger?

"Okay, Vic." She shook hands with him, which seemed silly after the steamy kiss they'd shared last night. Then again, this guy could make a handshake an erotic experience.

He gathered up a few tools he'd left on the ground and stuck them into the storage compartment on the back of his cycle. "If you really want to reward me for my hard work," he said, "I can think of ways that don't involve cash."

She gasped at his audacity.

"Have dinner with me," he added quickly before she could stomp off in a snit.

"I have to work late again," she said, almost grateful for the excuse. She wasn't ready for an entire evening alone with him.

"We'll make it a late dinner."

"How about lunch instead?" she hedged. Lunch seemed much less threatening. They could talk, get to know each other—

"I'll pick you up at ten tonight."

She would have protested, but he looked at her with such utter confidence that her objections withered. This was a man used to getting his way.

Without another word he left, climbing on board his cycle and rumbling off with a careless wave in her direction.

All right, so he was an alpha male. Such men made good leaders. They ran corporations and governments. They usually had all the women they could handle. One thing they didn't do was make good husbands, not for a woman who believed in equality between the sexes, mutual sharing and all that.

"He doesn't want to marry you," Angela grumbled to herself. If she took this thing any further, she had to face the fact that this was a man to enjoy fabulous sex with. Any further expectations on her part would be ludicrous.

She wasn't the type of person to have a fling. At least, she'd never been before. But maybe mind-blowing sex was something she ought to experience before she settled down to marriage, home and family, which she intended to do sometime in the next few years. Her friends certainly waxed enthusiastically about their various liaisons.

Talk about food for thought.

VIC HAD THE DAY OFF, but he stopped by the station to pick up his paycheck. Then out of habit he checked the bulletin board. The scores from the recent sergeant's exam, which Vic had taken, were still posted. He'd made a ninety-eight out of one hundred, the highest score of everybody who'd sat for the test. Just seeing that score after his name gave him a lift.

After the test he'd gone in for a personal assessment, interviewing with various people, and apparently he'd aced it. Rumor had it he was number one on "the list." Next time a sergeant's spot opened up, the promotion was his. He'd been a senior corporal for almost four years, and it was about damn time.

His mood deflated somewhat when he ran into Bobby Ray, who'd drawn desk duty while he recuperated from his injuries. Vic hadn't thought about what he would tell his partner about the previous night, but he doubted it would be the truth. He had no intention of turning a tomcat like Bobby loose on Angela. The woman was hot, in her own sweet way, and Vic intended to keep her all to himself. He couldn't remember the last time a woman had made him hard just standing there looking at him.

"Hey, buddy!" Bobby called to him from the bull-pen.

Damn. "I'm in kind of a hurry, Bobby."

"Just tell me how it went last night. Phoebe said this woman was hot looking but a real prude. Well, she didn't use those words, but I read between the lines."

Vic hesitated, then walked over to Bobby's temporary desk so everyone in the place couldn't overhear. "She wasn't bad." He didn't plan what he would say next. The words just poured out, seemingly of their own accord. "Her teeth were hardly noticeable as long as she kept her mouth closed."

"Teeth?"

"Oh, I guess Phoebe didn't tell you. Our gal's got quite an overbite. But it's kind of endearing, really."

"What about the rest of her? I mean, there's always a paper bag." Bobby guffawed, but Vic didn't join in.

"She's okay. From what she tells me, the diet center she goes to has really paid off. She says she has twenty pounds more to meet her goal, but I thought she looked fine."

"She's fat?"

"No. Well, not really huge or anything. Just normal size."

"Okay, okay, never mind that. What about her hands? How was her technique? I mean, she's a *massage therapist*."

Vic shook his head. "Her hands were fine, and I didn't even mind the smell that much."

"What smell?"

"It's this special medicinal lotion she uses for massage. She's allergic to the regular kinds. It smells kind of like mothballs, but it wasn't that strong."

Bobby's eyes bulged, and his lips drew into a grimace. "Did she put that stuff on *you?*"

"No, of course not. The scent of the lotion sticks to her, she said, no matter how many times she washes. I could smell it just standing next to her. Anyway, there was no massage. I just took her home, like I told you I would do."

"So you're telling me you didn't get lucky."

"It all depends on how you look at it." With that he left Bobby to mull over his own good luck. He felt only a twinge of guilt at the outrageous lies he'd told. Someday Bobby would probably talk to Phoebe and discover the truth, but Vic would deal with that when the time came.

A more immediate problem was what to do with Angela tonight—if she even let him through the door after the high-handed way he'd finagled a date from her. Ordinarily, for a late-night rendezvous, he would take a woman to a coffeehouse or sidewalk café for a bite to eat and some good conversation. But this situation with Angela demanded something unusual.

She definitely responded to an element of mystery. So he had to think of something unexpected, a little bit daring, a little risqué.

Did her building have a flat roof? he wondered.

ANGELA HATED EVERYTHING in her closet. Her clothes were so mundane, so ordinary, and much too conservative. Vic would be here in fifteen minutes, and she still wasn't dressed.

Finally she settled on her all-purpose spaghetti-strapped black dress. She could snazz it up with a beaded bolero vest and heels, or dress it down with a funky hat and lace-up boots, depending on where they were going. Whatever their destination, she would insist on driving. She couldn't negotiate the back of a motorcycle in a short dress.

She was ashamed of herself that she hadn't even considered not going. She *hated* it when a man had to have his way, when they brushed aside her ideas and suggestions as insignificant. Why, then, did those habits seem intriguing and exciting in Vic?

She'd always been independent, had never let anyone lead her around by the nose. Maybe it was the novelty of surrendering control, she reasoned as she debated over what color hose to wear. Black, maybe. She started to grab some black panty hose. Then she spotted a pair of stockings that required a garter belt.

Feeling naughty, she pulled them out of the drawer, running the smooth silk over the back of her hand.

She'd bought them on a whim and never worn them, but tonight seemed like a good time—they made her feel sexy. Not that she needed any artificial stimulation when Vic was around. She felt as if she could outsex Madonna when he looked at her with those electric blue eyes.

Angela didn't know what to do with her hair. Normally she wore it in a ponytail or braid, but that seemed too youthful for the way she felt tonight. She thought about pinning it up. Did guys ever really take a girl's hairpins out one by one so her hair could tumble over her shoulders, all sexy and tousled? She was afraid it wouldn't work in real life the way it did in movies, so she left her hair loose. She decided she liked the way the curled ends brushed her bare shoulders.

She was dressed and ready at ten minutes to ten. Since she hated watching the clock, waiting for a date to pick her up, she got to work on a neglected craft project, a cross-stitched pillow for a cousin who was getting married this summer. If Vic stood her up, at least she would have something to show for the evening.

The next time she looked up at the clock, it was ten-fifteen. She threw her needlework aside in disgust. The jerk had changed his mind!

It was for the better, she told herself. She had no business going out with a man like that. He was a threat to her well-ordered world, not to mention her sanity. She couldn't think rationally when he was around.

Just when she'd decided to change into her night-gown, a knock came at the door. Her heart jumped into her throat. If it was Vic, he ought to be ringing her from the front security door.

"Just a minute!" she called out, sliding her feet back into her black flats and zipping up her dress. If it was Vic, she'd give him an earful. Twenty minutes late, and not even a phone call to let her know.

Full of righteous indignation, she threw open the door, and any lecture she might have delivered died in her throat. Lord, the man was gorgeous, but in a tuxedo he was incredible. He didn't have that smooth, urbane James Bond look, but somehow he appeared oddly at ease in the formal wear. She wouldn't have expected that.

"How did you get through the security door?" she blurted out in the way of greeting.

"Your neighbor, Mrs. Gibbons, let me in."

Mrs. Gibbons? She was the old lady on the first floor who was terrified of burglars and muggers. She had three dead bolts on her door and required three pieces of ID before she'd let her own sister in. It was comforting to know that Angela wasn't the only female susceptible to Vic's charms.

"You look hot," Vic added, his voice husky.

A surge of feminine pleasure washed through her. She murmured her thanks, then moved aside to let him in. He looked out of place in her fussy, feminine living room, and she decided right then and there to redecorate. It looked as if a spinster lived here. She would use Vic as the focal point of the decor.

"Sit down, and I'll go change," she said. "I hadn't realized we were going formal."

He grabbed her arm before she could make good her escape. "You look just fine for where we're going."

"Oh, but I have this little beaded vest...." She didn't finish outlining her wardrobe possibilities to him. His hot gaze struck her absolutely dumb. Before she knew it he had his arms around her, and they were kissing.

It was a beautiful kiss, steamy, full of passion, yet oddly she knew it was just a kiss to be enjoyed for its own sake. This was a guy who knew how to kiss. He nipped at her lips, then moved in for the kill, covering her mouth with his, using a gentle but insistent pressure. He let his tongue flirt with hers, then just when she thought she was going to pass out from overwhelming sensations, he backed off to kiss her neck, her ear, her forehead.

He didn't press his advantage, for which she was grateful. She had hours yet to resist him.

Chapter Three

Angela eased away from Vic. "Let me get the vest anyway," she said. The husky breathlessness in her voice turned him on almost as much as the kiss had. "I want to look my best. Please sit down. I'll be right back."

He nodded, but he didn't sit. He'd figured out one of Angela's buttons—she liked to be in control. The less he allowed her to dictate to him, even with something as trivial as whether he should sit or stand, the more off balance she would be.

As she left the room, Vic contemplated her shapely legs, revealed to midthigh and encased in sheer black silk. He'd never seen her legs before, though he'd fantasized about them.

They were better than he'd dreamed, slender but with calf and thigh muscles clearly defined.

Vic had thought Angela looked quite sexy enough in her work clothes. There was something very sensual about her, a quality that would shine through even if she wore a nun's habit. But Angela in a short, figure-revealing black dress literally made his mouth go dry.

He hooked his thumbs into his pockets and paced around Angela's small living room, trying not to anticipate what the night might bring. Events were unfolding in surprising ways.

He hadn't planned on moving in for a kiss quite so abruptly, but the gesture had seemed as natural as breathing. She felt good in his arms; she fit perfectly against him, and as he'd pulled her close, he'd experienced a little thrill of victory—like when he'd been a kid and found a missing piece in a jigsaw puzzle, only lots, lots better.

How could one woman, a woman he hardly knew, have such an exaggerated effect on him? It wasn't just his body involved, but his mind, his spirit and, he was very much afraid, his heart.

Not that he was falling in love with her. He didn't allow himself to do that, not since college. In Vic's world, everything had its proper place. The problem with love was that it didn't like to stay in its place. It liked to ooze all over everything, spilling onto other parts of his sturdy, well-organized life until nothing functioned smoothly anymore.

Kimberly Rose Mundy, a woman he'd loved as thoroughly as any college kid can love, had turned his life into a circus. His grades had suffered, he'd shown up for his campus bookstore job late and disheveled, he'd neglected his friends, he'd dropped out of intramural basketball. She had consumed him.

Then, without preamble, Kimberly had dumped him for a med student.

He'd recovered quickly enough, pulling the shreds of his life back together before all was lost, mending fences and taking a hard look at the person he was before, during and after falling in love. After that, he'd managed to avoid the sticky emotion.

But Angela gave his heart palpitations nonetheless. He felt an undeniable, burgeoning affection for her, for her shy smile and the way she fought with herself over how to behave with him.

That was acceptable, he supposed. Affection was manageable. He wasn't sure what he wanted with Angela. He was a normal guy, so sex had to be part of the recipe, of course. Still, a fiery fling sounded appealing but unfulfilling somehow. Too shallow and confining for a woman like her.

A long-term friendship, perhaps, that included sex? He'd tried that before, a couple of times. He'd discovered that sooner or later the woman grew dissatisfied with the status quo and wanted to either deepen things or end it. He supposed that was the nature of a woman, to move in the direction of marriage. It wasn't, however, in his nature.

Did he need to know right now? He supposed not. He could wing this thing. That's what he'd been doing so far and it had worked out okay.

Angela reappeared shortly wearing the sparkly vest and a pair of spike heels that did great things to her already fabulous legs. "I'm ready if you are," she said breezily. "Unless you'd like a drink first? I have some box wine in the fridge...."

"No, I think we'd better go."

She grabbed a small purse and started for the front door, but he snagged her by the arm. "This way." He led her in the direction she'd just come from, where he assumed her bedroom was.

She dug in her heels. "What?"

"I'm not planning to drag you into the bedroom and ravish you, if that's what you thought," he said, smiling to soothe her expression of outrage. "A window in your bedroom leads to the fire escape. That's where we need to be."

She looked around, bewildered. "Why? Is the building on fire?" She smiled uncertainly.

Yeah, there was a fire, all right. Inside him. "All right, I guess I'll have to tell you. The fire escape leads up to the roof. That's where dinner is."

"You're kidding, right?"

In reply, he gestured for her to lead the way into her bedroom. "I'm completely serious."

Bewildered but wanting to be a good sport, she preceded him down a short hallway and into a bedroom. "You'll have to overlook the mess, okay?"

"I won't notice a thing," he promised.

But he did notice. Her double bed had been hastily made, with numerous fussy pillows with lace and satin trim heaped near the bentwood headboard. Several dresses and blouses were draped over a low chair, as if she'd tried on and discarded many outfits before deciding on the black dress. Instinctively he knew this was true, and the knowledge pleased him enormously.

Angela unlocked the window, but Vic stepped forward to raise it for her. It was large enough that they could step onto the tiny metal landing outside without contorting their bodies in undignified ways. Angela went first, sitting on the ledge, then swiveling those enticing legs through the opening. Her movements were graceful and feminine.

Vic followed, then closed the window. "After you," he said, gesturing toward a ladder attached to the brick wall leading up to the roof.

She folded her arms and gave him a sideways look. "Now you *have* to be kidding. I can't climb a ladder in this dress."

"Sure you can," he said easily. "Take your shoes off."

She stared at him a moment longer, challenging. He could tell she wanted to see what surprises he had planned for her on the roof, but this went against her conservative nature. Finally she capitulated, kicking off her shoes. "Okay, fine. But you go ahead of me. I don't want you looking up my dress. And you *would,* too. Don't try lying about it."

She was right. With a shrug he grabbed her shoes, stuck one in each pocket, then started up the ladder. When he reached the top, he climbed onto the roof and looked down. She was following, slowly, giving him a lovely view of her cleavage. It wasn't until then that Vic admitted to himself how afraid he'd been that she would balk at this crazy idea of his. He was knocking down her barriers one by one, but her personality was strong enough that victory was by no means assured.

He extended his hand and helped her the last few steps.

"I did it!" she said triumphantly once she was on firm footing. "That's the first time I ever climbed a ladder, other than a stepladder."

"I hope that's only one of many firsts tonight," he said as he set her shoes down for her to step back into.

She laughed, a bit hysterically he thought, then reclaimed her shoes.

The rooftop was dark, and they could actually see a sprinkling of stars in the navy blue sky, despite the fact they were in the middle of the city. A few blocks away the lights of Oak Lawn Avenue's late-night hot spots, muted through the treetops, provided a colorful backdrop. Farther into the distance, downtown Dallas's artfully lighted skyline shone like a jewel in the night.

"Oh, it's beautiful up here," Angela said, almost reverently. "I've been living in that apartment four years and I've never been on the roof before. It's isolated, but at the same time the city's life is all around."

Precisely why he'd chosen this environment. It was stimulating, yet still secluded. He took her arm and led her across the tar-and-gravel rooftop to a spot on the far side, where the branches of an enormous crepe myrtle tree brushed against the building, softening the harsh lines of the roof edge and gutters.

"Oh, my." Angela stopped in her tracks, admiring Vic's handiwork. A table covered with a white cloth bore two elegant place settings, courtesy of Vic's grandmother's dishes. He'd inherited them years ago, but they'd remained boxed up in his attic until today. Until now he'd never seen a need to go fancier than his sturdy stoneware and stainless.

The table was lit by a candle inside a glass, where the light breeze made it flicker. Off to the side was an ice bucket containing a good bottle of Chablis. Tucked under the table was a soft plastic container, similar to the ones the pizza delivery guys used to keep their pies warm.

"Sit down," Vic said. "Do you want some wine?"

"I'd love some," she replied, claiming one of the padded folding chairs at the table. "How did you get all this stuff up here?"

He'd about broken his back, that's how, hauling it all up that ladder, terrified the whole time that Angela would hear him creeping around on her fire escape and call the cops. Or if not Angela, one of her neighbors. He'd made sure to bring his ID shield just in case. But no one had questioned him or tried to stop him.

"Magic," he answered. He wanted her to think the task had been effortless.

As soon as he'd poured each of them a glass of wine, he went to the plastic container and began unpacking their dinner—first a small Caesar salad, then rosemary-tarragon breast of chicken, freshly grilled asparagus spears and crusty French bread.

"That smells wonderful," Angela said. "Don't tell me you cooked it."

He was tempted to lie. But he felt he'd been dishonest enough as it was. If he wanted more than this one night with her, he was going to have to start revealing a little of the real Vic Steadman. She might be bowled over by this dangerous mystery man, but he had a hunch she might actually like the real Vic, if he introduced him slowly.

"No, I can't claim cooking among my many skills. I got it from that gourmet-to-go place a few blocks from here."

"Great! I love their food."

She patiently allowed him to serve her. After Vic had filled their plates, and with mouthwatering aromas drifting up from the table, he took his own chair. He lifted his glass in a toast.

"To new experiences."

She lifted her own glass and tapped it against his with a smile and a nod. But an uneasy expression crossed her face. He wondered what bothered her about his toast.

During dinner, Vic questioned Angela about her job, her family, her hobbies. She was relaxed enough that she answered without hesitation. Whenever she made an attempt to steer the conversation toward him, he provided glib answers, then deftly reversed the flow once again.

He was glad to see that she had a healthy appetite.

Nothing irritated him like a woman who picked at a good dinner. Vic made sure her wineglass stayed full, though he carefully monitored how much she drank. For what he had in mind later, he wanted her relaxed but with a clear head.

He drank a couple of glasses himself, hoping it would take the edge off his own nerves. Though he felt he was performing with admirable suavity, he was a bundle of tension. Tonight mattered, more than it should, probably. He'd been too long without a woman, he reasoned. That was all it was.

"It hasn't escaped my attention that you don't like to talk about yourself," Angela said easily as he put away the leftovers.

He said nothing, hoping to distract her with his next assault on her taste buds, caramel cheesecake. Her eyes widened when he set the decadent wedge of dessert in front of her, but she didn't immediately dig in to it.

"An hour ago, when I was starving, you might have succeeded in distracting me with food, but not now. I've told you everything but my shoe size, and the only thing I know about you is that you ride a motorcycle, fix cars and you know how to bowl a woman over."

"What else do you need to know?" he said, shrugging playfully.

"Lots of stuff."

Vic sensed he wasn't going to wiggle off her hook this time. He sat down and took a bite of his cheesecake, savoring the sweet caramel flavor mixed with cool cream cheese. "My life's an open book," he said. "What do you want to know?"

"How many questions do I get?" she asked warily, obviously skeptical of his sudden openness. And well she should be, he thought guiltily.

"One. No, wait, two—okay, three. But that's my limit. I'm boring. Why would we want to talk about me?"

"What do you do for a living? Do you have a job?"

"That's two questions."

She narrowed her eyes at him, and he gave in.

"Okay, we'll count it as one." He paused, wondering if there was any way to make his job sound more mysterious. "Let's just say I associate with some of the city's less savory characters, and leave it at that."

"You're a criminal?" she asked, involuntarily pulling her chair back. *Uh-oh.* He'd gone too far.

"No, no. I'm a completely law-abiding citizen, I promise. It's just that my work isn't something a refined, beautiful woman such as yourself would want to hear about." And that, he decided, was probably the truth. Rounding up drunks, breaking up fights, writing tickets, patrolling high school football games for extra money when he was off duty—it just wasn't very glamorous. He was hoping to make sergeant soon, and he was fairly certain he would be assigned a detective position within the next couple of months. But he wasn't there yet.

"But you're employed? You're a contributing member of society?"

"Yes."

"You're annoyingly mysterious. How do you know I'm not interested in your job? I have very wide-ranging interests."

"Is that a question?"

"No. How many do I have left?"

"Two."

"Where do you live?"

"Near White Rock Lake." Which revealed very little. The old White Rock neighborhood featured everything from cramped apartments to mansions. "One more—make it a good one."

She paused and licked her lips. He was breathless, waiting for her next question, wondering what answers he could provide that would keep her off balance. It was a game. She knew it as well as he, or he wouldn't have continued with it.

When she finally voiced her next question, though, he was the one thrown off balance.

"Are you planning to make love to me tonight?"

Angela very nearly clamped her hand over her mouth. Where had that question come from? Some deep, *deep* part of her subconscious, no doubt. She'd been sitting there enjoying their banter, thinking what gorgeous blue eyes he had and how broad his shoulders looked in the tux.

She kept seeing quick images in her mind of her and Vic together—her fingers sifting through all that thick black hair, or slowly unfastening his bow tie and unbuttoning his shirt, then her kissing his chest.

Then her Question Number Three had popped out.

My Lord, she thought, *I just propositioned a man.* She'd never done that before, never even come close.

He didn't answer her right away. He stared back at her, one eyebrow cocked and a look of pure deviltry on his face. At least she hadn't shocked or disgusted him. Maybe she'd even excited him. Given her line of work, Angela knew a lot about body language. Vic didn't look agitated, but his rate of breathing had picked up.

"I think that's pretty much up to you," he finally said.

Then his answer was yes, she decided. All she had to do was make one move in his direction, and he was hers.

But she didn't move. A lifetime of caution kept her glued to the chair. *What about pregnancy?* she asked herself. She'd always thought that getting pregnant outside of marriage would be the worst disaster that could befall her. But the only thought that came to mind now was that it wouldn't be so bad having *his* baby.

What about her other fears surrounding sex? Losing her independence. Opening herself up to being hurt. Feeling foolish afterward. Being taken advantage of. When it came right down to it, she'd always been a little afraid that she simply wouldn't do it right, that her lack of experience would make her an inept, fumbling ninny.

Looking at Vic, she knew her independence was already at risk. He was quite capable of hurting her—all it would take would be for him to walk away after his conquest. She could feel more than foolish afterward.

But if anyone was taking advantage, it was Angela herself. And the way her instincts took over when she was with him, she couldn't envision herself as a clumsy lover. She would know what to do when the time came.

She tried to draw together every sensible thought in her repertoire about why making love with someone like Vic was a bad, bad idea. But somehow, the only sensible thought she could grab on to was, *There's an all-night drugstore around the corner, and it sells condoms.*

Without really meaning to, she pushed back her chair and stood. Her decision was made. And, really, it had been made the moment he walked in the door. She took a step toward him, then another; then she held out her hand.

She could have sworn his eyes sparkled with their own light. He took her hand and brought it to his lips, all the while staring into her eyes, mesmerizing her. He was magic, she decided.

Abruptly he stood up, so quickly that his chair fell back. Then she was in his arms again, her lips pressed against his in a kiss that caused her burgeoning passion to well up inside her like an overflowing well. Unlike the simpler kiss he'd bestowed upon her in the living room, this one was a prelude, brimming with promise. Vic held her face between his hands. She couldn't escape—not that she wanted to. Her mouth was his to pillage any way he desired, and he tried them all—hungry, devouring kisses that involved tongue and teeth and, she'd swear, tonsils, then light, teasing nips that left her limp and almost begging for more.

His grip on her loosened as he moved his lips along her jaw, to her ear, down her neck and to the hollow of her throat. His hands, meanwhile, explored her back in a proprietary manner that thrilled her. She had committed to him—her body, at least—and he was taking possession. He cupped her bottom with one large hand. The intimate contact ignited a fire deep within her core. She wanted him to touch her there and everywhere. She wanted to shed clothing and feel skin against skin. Never had she experienced such a strong drive to join her body with a man.

He moved his hands to the top of her dress and eased her vest off her shoulders, then slowly lowered the zipper. Cool night air caressed her back, followed quickly by Vic's touch against her bare skin, a new level of intimacy.

"I like your hair down," he said. "I can bury my face in it, and it smells like flowers."

"Thank you." She'd been noticing the way he smelled, too, like soap and menthol shaving cream, starch, and…yes, baby shampoo. As he kissed the sensitive place between her neck and shoulder, she pressed her nose into his hair and inhaled deeply. The scent reminded her of childhood and, oddly, of safety.

On some instinctive level she knew she was safe with Vic, no matter what outward appearances told her.

His talented hands moved to her shoulders and eased the spaghetti straps of her dress down her arms. Yes, all right, she was standing on her roof with nothing on above the waist but a strapless bra.

"I think—" she began, but he kissed her again.

"Don't think," he murmured.

"I won't change my mind. It's just that..." She couldn't articulate her thoughts into words when he laid those feathery kisses along her collarbone. She threw her head back and reveled in the new sensations, especially enjoying the feel of his soft lips on the tops of her breasts.

Her knees were getting weaker by the minute. She wanted to lie down with him, and if they'd been anywhere else but on the roof, she'd have given in to her impulse right there.

"Vic..."

"Mmm, what?" His words were muffled. He'd pressed his face against her breasts, teasing the cleft between them with his tongue. No one had ever done anything like that to her before.

"Um, uh, don't you...think...we should go...inside?" She couldn't seem to get enough air into her lungs.

"Uh-uh," he said as he moved his hands around to her back, seeking the clasp to her bra.

"But we can't...out here...."

"Sure we can. It's dark. No one can see us."

What he said was true. Out of the immediate sphere of the candle's glow, it was pretty dark. "But there's nowhere to lie down...."

"We don't have to lie down," he said, calmly knocking down her most pressing objection.

But no, she had one more. "Vic, we have to have protection." Ah, here was evidence she had not gone completely insane. On that one point she would not compromise, no matter how appealing the fantasy of bearing Vic's child might be.

By way of an answer he grasped her right hand and tucked it into the inside pocket of his tux jacket, where she felt a long string of square plastic packages.

"Good Lord, how many did you bring?"

He laughed, a low rumble that reminded her of his motorcycle. "Enough, I hope."

"So you planned this from the beginning." She wasn't sure whether she was supposed to be affronted by his premeditation or not.

He paused in his sensual assault and drew back, looking into her eyes with an honesty she hadn't seen before. "Sweetheart, I know you're naive in a lot of ways, but there's no way you could have recognized what went on here tonight as anything but a blatant seduction." His voice deepened until it was almost a whisper. "Yes, of course I planned for it. Believe me, there's nothing that throws a wet blanket over a seduction faster than having to make a midnight run to the 7-Eleven for condoms."

Angela laughed despite herself. This was the longest speech she'd ever managed to extract from him, and she got the distinct impression that she'd seen more of his true personality in those few words than he'd allowed her to glimpse before. His sense of humor was shining through. And the picture of him frantically throwing on clothes and making a mad dash to the convenience store...well, it was less than dignified and not in keeping with the controlled alpha male he'd presented to her so far.

And she liked it. Her affection for him expanded, making her chest feel almost too full.

She removed her hand from his pocket, letting it slide down around to his back. With one surprisingly coordinated flick of her wrist, she unfastened his cummerbund and let it fall at their feet.

His eyes smoldered, and her amusement fled. She leaned forward, draping her body against his, to whisper in his ear. ''I'd like to know how you're going to finish this seduction without us lying down.''

''I'll show you.''

Their conversation ground to a halt as once again they concerned themselves with exploring each other's bodies. Vic's jacket and tie joined his cummerbund in the gravel, but she left his shirt on, unbuttoned of course. She liked the contrast of the crisp, white cotton to his tanned chest.

As for her own clothes, the dress ended up around her ankles and the bra disappeared. Vic eyed her garter belt and lace-topped stockings with a low whistle. ''You had a few plans of your own, I see.''

She couldn't deny it. No matter what she'd told

herself about wanting to *feel* sexy, in the back of her mind she'd dressed for Vic.

For a long, almost terrifying moment, Vic just looked at her. She'd never stood half-naked for a man's inspection before, certainly not outdoors. But rather than making her nervous, his hot gaze inflamed her further. She could almost feel rays of desire pouring off him.

Impatience took hold of her. She reached for one of the garters, intending to dispense with the rest of her clothes while he watched.

"Stop."

"What?"

"The garter belt and stockings stay."

"But…" She was too embarrassed to say the rest. She couldn't remove her panties without removing the stockings first. Okay, if he was such an expert, let him figure out the logistics. She let go of the garter and simply stood there, her hands at her sides, waiting for his next move.

Without ever taking his gaze from her, he moved toward the dining table, picked up his knife and wiped it with his napkin.

Angela inhaled sharply. She wasn't scared, exactly. Deep down she knew this man would not do her physical harm. But that dangerous sparkle in his eyes thrilled her almost to the point of dizziness.

He sauntered back to her with the knife. With one hand he pulled at the lace edge of her panties, holding them out from her body right at the hipbone. The cold steel of the knife brushed her skin, a dramatic contrast to the heat of his touch. Then, with a casual flick, he cut the black silk, which fell away from her body.

Okay, so he was very good at logistics. He tossed the knife aside, then pulled her into his arms again, caressing her bare bottom and allowing her to feel his hardness pressing against her.

"Those were very expensive panties," she objected feebly.

"I'll buy you more."

When he kissed her again, her knees, which had been wobbly for the past fifteen minutes, finally gave way. She would have fallen if he hadn't held her up, one hand finding a very intimate handhold.

"We need a bed." She tried again.

"We don't," he insisted, maneuvering her until he had her leaned up against a chimney. The cool, coarse brick against her bare back was yet a new sensation. She managed to stand there under her own power for a few moments while Vic removed the rest of his clothes.

When he started to shrug out of his shirt, she stopped him. "The shirt stays," she said, mirroring the order he'd given her a minute ago. She fully expected him to ignore her wishes, as he'd done so often. But he gave her a knowing look and left the shirt on.

She had avoided looking directly at his manhood, but now she couldn't help herself. He was magnificent and large and not a little threatening. All at once those doubts she'd managed to keep at bay assailed her.

Being deflowered was painful. Every single one of her friends had mentioned that fact. Whether the event was hurried or slow, with a considerate lover or a fumbling jackass, it hurt. The fact that she really, really wanted to do this wouldn't make any difference.

She should tell him, she realized. But what if that changed everything?

He came to her and kissed her, tenderly, sweetly, and her doubts melted. Like everything else tonight, the issue of her virginity would work itself out. She would know when the right time was.

Vic kissed her breasts, first one, then the other, reviving her passion to a fever pitch. Without words he pressed a condom packet into her hand. Though she'd never touched one in her life, except at Sarah's bachelorette party, theoretically she knew what to do with it. She tore the package open with her teeth and removed the thin sheath. Taking a huge, deep breath for courage, she reached down and, without even looking, performed the task perfectly. Beginner's luck.

Vic gasped at her first touch, but she wasn't unaffected herself. He was so hot and hard. And suddenly she couldn't wait to have him inside her.

"I'm ready, Vic. Please, now."

He needed no further encouragement. He grasped her around the waist and swiveled her so that his back was against the chimney. Then he lifted her, and with admirable control, slowly lowered her onto his shaft.

The fullness was pleasant at first, until he met her

resistance. He obviously felt it, too, because he gave her a questioning look, as if he couldn't quite believe what he was experiencing.

"Yes, I'm a virgin," she said, her eyes filling with tears from the emotion overcoming her.

"You're *what?*"

"Don't stop!" With that she took over, pulling him into her with one deep thrust.

Chapter Four

Vic was a man torn in two. He was buried inside a beautiful, sexy, willing woman who turned him on in ways he couldn't even describe. But that woman had tears in her eyes.

"God, Angela..."

"Please, don't stop," she said again, wiggling against him in a way that ensured he couldn't stop if he wanted to. It wasn't as if he could undo the past thirty seconds, anyway. He'd just deflowered a virgin.

Grasping her around the hips, he moved her slowly, gently, up and down his shaft, creating exquisite sensations that challenged his control. "Am I hurting you?"

"No," she said hastily. Then she laughed as the tears spilled out of her eyes. "Well, a little, maybe. But it feels good, too. Oh, Vic..."

He saw something in her eyes besides tears, something hard to describe. It was as if he was seeing inside her soul. She was opening to him, giving him something more precious than even her virginity.

He felt dizzy at the realization of what he'd done.

He'd taken something from Angela through deception.

Then he couldn't think anymore, because she'd wrapped her arms around his shoulders and was moving against him in a way no virgin should have known how to do so perfectly. He could do nothing but respond, answering her with thrusts that went deeper and deeper.

Angela moaned and threw her head back. Moisture still glistened on her cheeks, but the tears were drying and no more followed. She was moved by passion now, not pain.

Moments later she let herself go. She did it quietly—no showy screams of ecstasy—but Vic felt her climax in his own body, felt her accelerated breathing and that exquisite moment when all the tension released itself.

He hadn't even realized he'd been holding himself back until then. With one last thrust he took his own pleasure, wrapping his arms tightly around Angela's body and burying his face in her cloud of dark hair.

When it was all over, they clung to each other as the sights and sounds and smells of the city around them gradually came back into focus.

Bobby Ray had said Angela was repressed, that she hardly ever dated, but no one had said anything about her being a virgin. If he'd known…if only she'd told him earlier. He never would have come on so strong. He would have given her every opportunity to change her mind instead of trying to overwhelm her senses.

Guilt washed over him like a waterfall.

"Why didn't you tell me?" he finally asked in a hoarse voice.

"I didn't want you to change your mind." She laughed a little. "Does it have to be such a big deal?"

Vic eased their bodies apart, wondering now if this rooftop had been such a hot idea. He wanted to hold Angela in his arms, to reassure her as he imagined she needed reassurance right now. Instead they were reduced to searching for their discarded clothes while gravel bit into bare feet.

He kissed her lightly before bending to retrieve her dress and handing it to her. "It's a little unusual for me, is all."

"Exactly. Men like you run from virgins. So I didn't tell you. I'm sorry for not being honest."

Sorry? She was sorry? She stood there before him, gloriously almost naked, making no move to cover herself. She held the forgotten dress in one hand and looked down at her stocking toes.

"Angela."

She looked up.

"You don't have to apologize for giving me an incredible gift, okay?" He was the one who should be apologizing. But before he could say he was sorry for deceiving her, he would have to confess about Bobby and the fix-up and the sabotaged car. He suspected she wouldn't take kindly to it, so he kept his mouth shut. For now.

It was hard to tell in the darkness, but it looked as if she might be blushing. She turned away and shook out the dress so she could step back into it. Vic took the opportunity to throw on his own clothes.

Say something, he silently urged her. She remained maddeningly pensive.

"Why me?" he finally asked as he sat down to put on his shoes.

"Why not?" she answered glibly, picking up her bra and the ruined panties. She wadded the undergarments into a ball, then searched around for somewhere to put them. Finally she dropped them again with a sigh.

"Because a beautiful woman doesn't get to be your age without having sex unless she's waiting for something very specific." And Vic wanted to know what it was, so he could keep doing it.

When she didn't answer, he held out his hand to her. "Come here, please." She did, almost reluctantly. As soon as he could reach her, he pulled her into his lap, settled her head on his shoulder and wrapped his arms around her. "Was it like you imagined it would be?"

"Not exactly."

"Was it better or worse?" He held his breath, waiting for her answer. No guy wanted to hear that his sexual performance had been a disappointment.

"Do we have to talk about it?"

"No, of course not." Stupid, really, for him to be interrogating her. He'd never done that with a woman before. He couldn't remember needing ego strokes before. Then again, he'd never physically hurt a woman while making love to her.

She shivered, and he rubbed her bare arms. "Are you ready to go inside now?"

"We can't leave this mess up here. All these dishes—"

"I'll take care of it later."

Finally he earned a smile from her. "A man who does the dishes. You truly are a woman's fantasy."

At the word *fantasy,* Vic's conscience gave him a painful tweak. He'd done his job, done it perhaps too well. Angela's well-meaning friends had wanted her to experience a fantasy that would sweep her off her feet. He'd done just that. But had he done her a disservice? The man she'd made love to was a sham, hardly any more substantial than a figment of her imagination. The mysterious Vic Steadman she'd been so enthralled with was a pretty far cry from his true personality.

He had to tell her the truth. He knew that. But did it have to be now, while she was dealing with so many other things?

Making a decision, he swept her into his arms and carried her to the edge of the roof where the fire escape was. If he told her about the blind-date setup now, he risked her kicking him out of her life forever. And that was something he absolutely didn't want. Angela was special, different, and he definitely wanted to get to know her. Tonight he would figure out how to break the news to her that he was really just a regular guy with a paycheck and a mortgage, carrying around his own flaws and insecurities. Tomorrow would be soon enough to actually do it.

ANGELA BREATHED A SIGH of relief after she and Vic somehow got down the fire escape and through her bedroom window. She felt less overwhelmed now that she was surrounded by her familiar things. This was the real world. She wasn't caught up in some fantasy of moonlight and soft spring breezes; she was just a woman who'd made love to a man.

A fabulous, sexy man, gentle, caring, everything she'd ever dreamed of. If that wasn't fantasy…

Now they stood in her frilly, cluttered bedroom, just inches from her bed. What to do, what to do?

He smiled, that wicked, crooked smile that made her insides go all squiggly. Sated though she'd been a few scant minutes ago, her lust for this man was hardly pacified. Just thinking about what he'd done to her, with her, caused that now-familiar coil of heat to start up deep inside her.

This would never do. She had to get control of herself. It wouldn't be wise to throw herself into a full-fledged relationship with Vic when she knew so little about him. She had to think, to plan, and most important, she needed to know her own heart.

"Would you understand," she began, "if I wanted to be alone?"

He looked startled, but he quickly covered up that reaction. "Of course. You have to work in the morning, I imagine."

She nodded.

Then he grabbed both of her hands in his. "Thank you, Angela, for an evening I'll never forget. I mean that." He drew her to him and kissed her gently, almost respectfully, and then he was gone, ducking through the window and vanishing into the night like some superhero. She immediately felt bereft, and she had second thoughts about sending him away.

Angela closed the window, drew the blinds, then peeled off her clothes and collapsed onto the bed.

She'd sent him away because she'd needed time to think about what had just happened, to savor it, to wonder at it, and to etch every glorious moment of it into her memory. If she could have orchestrated her first time down to the nth detail, it never could have been as perfect as making love to Vic. Sure, there had been some pain. Big deal. Any discomfort had quickly been overshadowed by other feelings, physical sensations unlike anything in her experience or imagination.

Then there was that other aspect, the thing she could only describe as spiritual, and she'd been completely unprepared for it. When she'd been joined with Vic, she'd felt open to him, vulnerable, completely trusting. It felt as if he could see inside her, that he'd been free to examine every nuance of her psyche, every secret she harbored.

He hadn't judged her. Instead, he had accepted everything about her. The experience had been both freeing and a little frightening. She would remember that spiritual bonding long after the physical sensations slid into the murkier depths of memory.

She should take a shower, she thought. But Vic's scent remained on her skin, and she didn't want to wash it away just yet. She wondered if he would have stayed the night if she'd asked him to. She pictured them awakening, rumpled and drowsy, and making love again, taking their time. Maybe sharing a quick cup of coffee and the morning paper before she hurried off to work.

"And you sent him home, you idiot," she said aloud. Why had she done that? What if she never saw him again? She didn't know how to get in touch with him. He didn't have her phone number. He'd made his conquest, and now he might very well move on, find some other naive woman on whom to work his wiles.

She realized she could drive herself crazy. She also realized she'd been right all along. Making love to a man outside of a serious, committed relationship opened her up to all kinds of insecurities and unpleasantness.

But was she having regrets? Second thoughts?

No way.

ANGELA WAS LATE TO WORK the next day, something that was almost unheard of. As soon as she walked in the door, Terri handed her two pink message slips. Angela nearly ripped them out of the poor receptionist's hands, her heart soaring as she visually scoured the messages for Vic's name, then plummeting when she realized the calls were only from clients wanting to reschedule.

Phoebe challenged Angela at her office door. "You're late."

"My first client isn't until ten," Angela started to say, but Phoebe cut her off.

"Oh, for heaven's sake, Angie, I wasn't scolding. You know we don't punch a clock around here. I was just wondering if everything was…okay?"

Angie opened her office door and went inside. "Everything's fine. I just overslept."

"Late night?"

Angela all but gasped. How did Phoebe know? She hadn't said a word yesterday about her late date. No one had seen her in the parking lot with Vic yesterday. Was her first serious sexual experience branded onto her forehead?

Phoebe's eyes widened. "I knew it! You had a date, didn't you?"

"Well, sort of." She couldn't help but smile.

"The guy who rescued you the other night. I *thought* something was going on there. You don't have an impulsive bone in your body, but you let that guy take you home. He must be some looker."

"He's okay." Just the best-looking, sexiest guy she'd ever met. But she wasn't ready to share him yet. For now, he was hers and hers alone. And if he was gone from her life forever, he would remain only hers. A searing memory of the most fantastic deflowering any girl ever had. The telling of it would diminish it, she knew. And anyway, her dealings with Vic were no one's business but her own. Just because her friends had no shame, spilling their guts about embarrassing sexual encounters, that didn't mean she had to.

Phoebe shrugged, turned to leave, then stopped. "Oh, Dr. Nausbaum said to remind you about the Women's Expo. You can make it, right?"

Relieved to be on a safer topic, Angela checked her calendar. "Yes, I'm free that whole weekend." In her precise handwriting she wrote down the engagement. Dr. Sylvia Nausbaum, who was majority owner of the Be Well Clinic and the closest thing Angela had to a boss, was a firm believer in getting out into the community to share information about their unique approach to healing. This would be the third year they'd participated in the huge trade show, and Angela, with her five-dollar chair massages, was always the star attraction. She loved doing it, and the money went to charity.

Phoebe loitered in the doorway, looking as if she wanted to say something else. Angela did her best to ignore her.

"C'mon, Angie, give. What happened?"

Angela sighed and closed her date book. "We had dinner. We talked. We parted company around midnight. End of story." She smiled again. She couldn't help it.

"So, is he gonna call?"

Angela tried to sound casual. "Heck if I know."

"Well, jeez, Angie, you're supposed to find these things out before you let the guy escape. Get a firm commitment."

"I didn't want to do that."

"You didn't like him?"

"I liked him, all right? I didn't want to push."

Phoebe pursed her lips. "You really don't know how to play this game, do you?"

Angela was appalled at the idea that building a relationship was some game. To her it was serious business. Any decisions a woman made about a boyfriend, a lover, a husband had a profound effect on her life.

She reopened her appointment book and started making notations. "Can we drop this, please?" If Phoebe kept pushing, Angela knew she would spill everything, including how Vic had cut her panties off with a knife. Wouldn't *that* produce some oohs and aahs.

Phoebe's face fell. "Yeah, sure. Want to do lunch at Gordo's?"

"I'll probably work through lunch." Angela was grateful to have such a handy excuse. She didn't think she could handle any more interrogations from her well-meaning friends.

PHOEBE, VICTORIA, TERRI and Sarah sat crowded around one of the tiny tables at Gordo's sharing a large pepperoni and pineapple.

"So why didn't Angie come to lunch with us?" Victoria asked, picking all the pepperoni off the one slice of pizza she allowed herself.

"Said she had to work," Phoebe said with a snort. "Terri, you have the master schedule. Did she have any clients scheduled for midday?"

"Nothing till two," Terri said. "What's with her, anyway? All morning long she was so distracted she wouldn't even answer the intercom."

"Head in the clouds," Victoria added.

"She couldn't remember any of her patients' names," Sarah put in. "Kept calling Mrs. Anderson 'Mrs. Atkinson.'"

"Wow, that's not like her." Victoria took a sip of her diet Coke and delicately blotted her mouth. "Maybe we should talk to her."

"Maybe," Phoebe said. "But maybe we should talk to Bobby Ray."

The other three women froze and stared at Phoebe curiously.

Finally Terri spoke.

"I thought he took her home and it was no big deal."

"They went out last night," Phoebe said, relishing her bit of gossip. "But she wouldn't give me any details, darn it."

Sarah gasped. "Why didn't she tell us? Oh, my God, what if it was such a horrible experience she can't bring herself to talk about it?"

Terri took out her cell phone. "Let's call Bobby Ray. If he laid a hand on her—"

"That was the point," Phoebe reminded her friend, taking the phone. "Still, I think we should get his side of it." She pulled up the antenna and dialed her cousin's phone number. But it rang and rang. He apparently hadn't turned on his answering machine.

"No luck."

Suddenly no one could eat their pizza.

"What if we did something bad?" Sarah asked, voicing the fear they all were harboring. "What if we meddled in Angela's life, and she got hurt some-how?''

"Bobby wouldn't hurt her," Phoebe said, defending her cousin.

"Not on purpose," Victoria agreed. "But Angie's pretty sensitive."

"And naive," Terri put in. "It wouldn't take much to hurt her."

"We better talk to her," Sarah said. "We gotta square things with her."

The others agreed, though uneasily.

ANGELA ATE A COUPLE of granola bars for lunch, then got down on the floor of her office and did a few yoga stretches. Her body was sore in places she'd never imagined she could hurt, but it was a good kind of pain.

The other pain, the one inside her chest, wasn't so good. Vic hadn't called. He hadn't sent flowers or candy. Isn't that what guys did after they made love? Or was that only in old movies?

If her sexual naiveté had bored him to tears and he never intended to see her again, she would understand, but she wished he would let her know so she could write him off and move on.

Yeah, write him off. Like that was going to happen this century.

A tentative tapping came on her door. It was early for the others to be back from Gordo's, and it wouldn't be Sylvia, who was manning the front desk during lunch. That was the cool thing about the Be

Well Clinic, which offered a combination of traditional and alternative treatments for pain. Though each of the partners had invested different amounts of money in the venture, they were all equal in status. Everyone pitched in, no one was too proud.

Angela pushed herself to her feet and opened the door, surprised to see her four friends crowded into the hallway, every one of them looking penitent.

"We have to talk to you," Phoebe said.

Ten minutes later, all of them sitting in the break room, Angela could hardly believe the story her co-workers had confessed to her.

"We were only trying to help."

"You said you'd never been swept away."

"You refuse regular blind dates."

"My cousin's really a nice guy. I wouldn't set you up with a jerk."

All of their excuses made no difference. Angela felt thoroughly manipulated, a complete fool. She should have known it was too good to be true. She'd thought Vic was her fantasy man...well, he was. His behavior had been calculated to push her buttons, and he'd succeeded all too well.

No wonder he hadn't called. Vic was little better than a gigolo. Or maybe he *was* a gigolo.

Angela had to ask. "You didn't...didn't actually pay him, did you?"

Phoebe's quick, emphatic denial put that suspicion to rest, at least. "He wanted to meet you," she went on. "It wasn't like I had to twist his arm." She hesitated. ''I did promise to spring for the beer and pizza next party. So, how was it? Did you really like him?''

Angela said nothing. She was too stunned to cry, though that was what she wanted to do.

''Did you at least think he was cute?'' Terri asked. Cute? Vic?

''Did you have any fun at all?'' Victoria asked impatiently, earning stern glares from the others.

''Oh, yeah, I had fun,'' Angela said. ''A lot of fun. In fact, one of the best nights of my life.'' Her friends started to smile, but she continued relentlessly. ''Because I thought this great, sexy, mysterious guy was so attracted to me that he would go to any lengths to have me. Because I was flattered that any guy, much less this dreamy guy on a motorcycle, would pursue me so relentlessly. Because I dared to think there just might be something special, something once-in-a-lifetime happening between us.''

She paused and stared at the other women, stared at each one in turn until they were forced to look away.

''Because I opened myself up in a way I never would have done if I'd known the whole thing was a setup.''

''When you say, 'opened myself up,''' Phoebe began, but Angela cut her off.

''Sex might be just a game to all of you, but it isn't to me. Keep that in mind next time you go meddling in my life.''

Angela fled the break room and made a beeline for her office, nearly running over Beryl, the clinic's nutritionist, in her haste. After closing and locking her office door, she let her tears flow.

She was such a fool, such a naive, silly thing. How could she have let herself be taken in so easily? She could just imagine what Vic had said when Phoebe approached him. "Yeah, sure, I'll show her a good time. But you'll owe me." Or maybe he'd been challenged by the fact that she was a virgin. Some challenge. She'd stood about as firm as a bowl of pudding.

She supposed she should be grateful he'd shown her some consideration after the deed was done. At least he'd been gentle, said the right words, acted as if there might really be some affection behind the lust.

Somehow she got through the rest of her patients, even managing to smile and offer pleasantries. But every free moment she brooded about her date with Vic, replayed it, wrote herself new dialogue, made herself more sophisticated.

Well, the night couldn't be undone, she thought as she straightened her desk after the last patient had left. It was early, but she decided she would slip out so she wouldn't have to face Phoebe and company again.

In truth, her virginity had been rather tedious. She was glad she'd ended it. She owed Vic her gratitude, really.

But gratitude was about the last emotion to come to mind when she came out into the parking lot and saw who was leaning against her car.

Chapter Five

Vic was loitering in the parking lot like an obsessed stalker when Angela came out to her car. He didn't see her until she was right in front of him, because he'd been busily involved in a fantasy. In fact, he'd been leading an active fantasy life all day, fueled by memories of his incredible evening with Angela.

His shift had mercifully ended at three. He'd showered and changed clothes and come straight here. He could have just called Angela at the clinic, now that he remembered the name. But that would have given her the opportunity to turn him down. He wasn't taking any chances.

It was only four o'clock, and he hadn't expected Angela to materialize in the parking lot quite this early. So she'd caught him staring off into space, thinking about his fantasy woman come to life in black silk stockings, licking her full, pink mouth, her eyes all smoky with desire.

At the moment, however, her eyes were anything but smoky. In fact, he could have sworn they were shooting sparks.

''What are you doing here?'' she asked without a hint of welcome in her voice.

Vic sensed there might not be a right answer to her question. ''Coming to see you?''

''Yeah, right. And what did Phoebe offer you this time?''

''Huh?''

''The beer and pizza wasn't enough? Did you hit her up for caviar and champagne this time?''

''Angela, what in hell are you talking about?''

''The jig's up, Vic. You don't have to pretend all this smarmy devotion anymore. You did your job and you did it well. Would you move away from my door, please? I'd like to get in my car.''

Vic didn't budge. ''Not until you explain.''

''Explain why I'm mad? Maybe because I don't like to be made a fool of. Maybe because I prefer for a guy to ask me out because he likes me, not because he likes pizza.''

''I *don't* like pizza.'' And sometimes he thought he was the only human who didn't.

''And *maybe* because I would have preferred for my first time to be with someone who hadn't been bribed to go out with me! Now, *let me into my car.*''

He didn't dare deny her. She had that look in her eye, like his mother's cat when it had tired of petting and wanted to be left alone. One more tummy tickle, and *wham!* Iodine and butterfly bandages all over his hand.

He stepped out of Angela's way, but while she was stowing her purse and tote bag behind the driver's seat, he calmly walked to the other side of her car and climbed in through the passenger door.

She didn't notice him sitting there until she'd gotten in herself. Then she stared at him, her eyes mere slits. "Can you not take a hint?"

"I want to know what I did wrong."

"What do you think? Your cousin Phoebe sabotaged my car, then coerced you into 'rescuing' me and seducing me."

"I don't have a cousin Phoebe."

"Are you telling me you were in the parking lot two nights ago completely by chance?"

He didn't want to compound his sins now by lying. "Well, no. Not completely."

"Case closed. Now leave me alone."

"Angela, no guy in his right mind would have to be bribed to take you out on a date. Or to make love to you. Yeah, okay, you were set up. But if I *had* met you by chance, I'd have pursued you. I'd have done everything in my power to bowl you over. From the moment I saw you, I wanted you."

He could see he wasn't getting through to her. She sat behind the wheel, ramrod straight, jaw clenched, fists balled up. "Forgive me if I'm a little skeptical. You've lied about everything else. You could have fixed my car in five seconds by screwing the distributor cap back on."

She was right on that score. "I guess I don't blame you for being angry, but—"

"Get out of my car before I call a cop."

"I *am* a cop."

"No, you're not. You're a mobster or something. Maybe a Hell's Angel."

He knew he'd never get through to her till she stopped being so angry. Maybe he could reach her through humor. "The Hell's Angels are all old, fat and bald by now."

She didn't so much as crack a smile. "Out!"

"Yes, ma'am." He opened the car door. "Would it help if I said you're beautiful when you're angry?"

She threw her key chain at him. He dodged it just in time, then slid out of the car. But he couldn't resist a parting shot. "I don't suppose you'd give me your phone number?"

In answer she started up the engine and punched the gas, the passenger door flapping open and closed until she turned a corner and it latched.

"Well, that didn't go very well," he murmured.

Since Vic was a cop, it wasn't that hard for him to track down Angela's phone number. He left a message on her answering machine that evening. Thirty minutes later, he tried again, but the machine didn't pick up. He figured she'd unplugged the phone.

Man, she was madder than a whole hill full of fire ants. He needed a new strategy. He needed to talk to Bobby Ray. Bobby's girlfriends were always getting mad at him, and he seemed to know how to handle it.

ANGELA TRIED TO HOLD ON to her anger the next morning, but it was hard to stay mad at the bunch she worked with.

First there was an "I'm sorry" balloon tied to her office doorknob. Then there was the mountain of 3 Musketeers bars—her favorite—sitting on her desk. Beneath the candy bars was a gift certificate for a half day at the Neiman-Marcus spa.

Since she'd skipped breakfast, she ripped open one of the candy bars and dug in. Nothing like chocolate to soothe a bad mood. Maybe if she ate ten or fifteen of the tasty little morsels…

She'd left her door open a crack, which around this clinic was an invitation. Before long, Phoebe was peeking in.

"Angie? Are you talking to me?"

"Maybe," Angela replied. She wasn't going to make this too easy for her conspiratorial friends.

"'Cause if the candy bars aren't working, I want them back."

Angela gathered all the candy protectively in the circle of her arms. "No way. They're mine, I earned them and I'm eating all of them myself."

Phoebe laughed, and Angela smiled a tiny bit herself. It felt good. "Oh, come in."

Phoebe opened the door. Behind her were Victoria, Sarah and Terri. And they all talked at once.

"We're really sorry, Angie."

"We didn't mean to hurt you."

"We thought you'd like it."

"It seemed like a good idea at the time."

And finally their voices coalesced into one predominating question. "What happened?"

Victoria and Phoebe pulled up chairs. Sarah

perched herself on the massage table, and Terri sat cross-legged on the floor.

"I've been trying to call my cousin," Phoebe said, "but he must be out of town or something. But I swear, if he hurt you or insulted you or caused you any grief—"

"He didn't," Angela said. "He did everything you asked him to. He rescued me, and then he swept me off my feet and so overwhelmed me that—" She cut herself off before any more of her confession could tumble out. She didn't want anyone to know what had happened. At the same time, part of her wanted to confide in someone, to commiserate, to have someone reassure her that the pain she was feeling in her chest would fade with time.

"That what?" Terri asked breathlessly.

"Well, that I lost all my good judgment, that's all."

Apparently her comment was completely transparent, because Phoebe punched a fist in the air. "Atta girl!"

Angela felt her face heating up as the others barraged her with questions.

"Was it good?"

"Did he buy dinner?"

"Did he stay till morning?"

"Did you use birth control?"

"When are you seeing him again?"

Angela felt herself losing patience. They still didn't realize what they'd done to her, how cheap they'd made her feel. "Yes, yes, no, yes and never."

They busily calculated in their minds which answer went with which question, then stopped and stared, dumbfounded. "Never?" they asked in unison.

"How do you even know he wants to see me again?" Angela countered.

"Why wouldn't he?"

"Maybe because you can't keep ponying up for pizza and beer every time we go out?"

Phoebe sighed impatiently. "Angie, it wasn't like that at all. No one has to bribe Bobby Ray to go out with an attractive woman. Anyway, the deal was for him to rescue you. Then, if he liked you, he could proceed on his own from there. No one was twisting his arm to—"

"What did you say?" Angela asked. Her heart had all but stopped beating.

"I said the deal was for him—"

"No, before that."

"Um, I think I said that no one has to bribe Bobby Ray—"

"Stop. Who's Bobby Ray?"

"My cousin!"

"The guy who picked me up in the parking lot— he said his name was Vic. Vic Steadman."

The others looked at each other, bewildered. Finally Terri spoke. "Who the hell is Vic Steadman?"

Phoebe repeated the name to herself several times, trying to place it. "Wait, I know. Vic Steadman is Bobby Ray's partner."

"What kind of partner?" Angela wanted to know. "Do they own a business or something?" She had a hard time picturing Vic running a dry cleaning business or a convenience store.

"They're cops," Phoebe said. "Didn't he tell you that?"

He had, she realized. The day before, when she'd been threatening to call the police. She'd thought he was lying. But he'd been telling the truth—maybe about everything. He didn't have a cousin named Phoebe. And he didn't even like pizza.

This shed a new light on things.

The phone buzzed, and Terri hopped up and rushed to her post at the front desk. It was past eight, and she probably hadn't yet unlocked the front door.

The others scooted out to tend to their own duties—all but Phoebe. "So what do you think happened?"

"Apparently Bobby Ray had second thoughts about a blind date with a repressed spinster—"

"I never told him you were a repressed spinster."

"Well, you must have hinted at something like that. So he conned his partner into filling in."

"I can't believe he did that. Bobby knows I'd kill him for setting you up with a stranger."

"Maybe that's why he's not answering his phone."

Phoebe frowned and pushed up her sleeves. "I'll get to the bottom of this."

"Maybe you'd better just let it alone."

"But—"

"Please."

Phoebe relented. "Okay, if that's what you want."

She gave Angela a quick hug, then left as Angela's first patient arrived.

"TALK TO YOUR COUSIN," Vic said to Bobby Ray later that day as they changed clothes at the end of their shift. "Get her to convince Angela I'm not some gigolo. Otherwise I'm toast."

"I thought you said she was fat and ugly," Bobby said, eyes narrowed suspiciously.

"That was to keep you off the scent."

"Then she was hot?"

"Yeah, she's very pretty, okay?"

"Did you get any?"

Vic clenched his jaw and focused on buttoning up his shirt. He'd never been the kind of guy who bragged about sexual exploits, not since the sixth grade when he'd told all of his buddies about kissing Janice Porter, only to have her brother track him down after school and beat him up.

"You didn't! Hah, you struck out, and with a girl who's desperate for it."

Vic chose to let his obnoxious partner think what he liked. "Will you talk to your cousin or not?"

"Yeah, sure, I'll call Phoebe."

But Vic didn't like that speculative gleam in Bobby Ray's eyes. He couldn't help wondering if he'd just made a huge tactical error.

ANGELA PLANNED TO SPEND the weekend quietly— eating out at her favorite little cafés, reading, maybe renting some videos. Action movies, though, no romances. A blinking light on her answering machine foiled her plans.

It might be her mother, she thought. Or one of any number of friends. Or a sales call. Or it might be Vic.

Angela nearly broke a fingernail pushing the ''play messages'' button.

''Hey, Angela. This is Bobby Ray Allen, Phoebe's cousin. I was supposed to meet you the other night, but I got hit over the head with a beer bottle. I told Vic to make sure you got home safely, but I guess he got a little carried away with the job. Anyway, I'd like a chance to make it up to you. Gimme a call.'' He rattled off a number.

Angela fell into her overstuffed chair, filled with mixed feelings. Bobby Ray sounded kind of cute. He had a smooth Southern drawl and a way with words. But she didn't want to meet any more men right now. Maybe if he'd been the one to rescue her...

She couldn't even imagine it. If any man besides Vic Steadman had approached her in that parking lot, she was sure she would have run screaming into the night.

So, Vic had taken over for his injured partner. It was noble, really. Still, he could have told her the truth about how he came to be in that parking lot. She abhorred lying or subterfuge of any sort.

On the other hand, these new circumstances meant that Vic had been under no pressure to flirt with her, ask her out, or make love to her. He'd done that all on his own.

The realization gave her a warm feeling all over.

She hadn't been some charity case. He'd been genuinely attracted to her. The elaborate seduction had been his idea.

The surge of happiness was followed quickly by despair. She'd driven him off. She cringed as she recalled her shrewish screams at him, how she'd brushed off his attempts to smooth over the rough spots. He was probably glad to be rid of her!

She didn't even know his phone number, and it wouldn't be in the book. Cops never put their numbers in the book. But she did have his partner's. She played the message back and dialed the number as Bobby Ray rattled it off.

"Bobby Ray," she said when a male voice answered, "this is Angela Capria."

"Angela." His voice immediately sank a couple of notches, to what she guessed was supposed to be sexy. She thought it a trifle comical.

Angela offered to meet Bobby Ray that night at Starbucks for an after-dinner coffee. Her plan was to explain to him that she'd been pretty hard on poor ol' Vic, and that she wanted to apologize to him.

Bobby had said on the phone he wanted only to make amends for the mix-up, and she'd believed him. But as they sat together at a small table in a dark corner of the Starbucks patio, sipping cappuccinos, she discovered that Bobby Ray had more hands than an entire fraternity house. If he wasn't squeezing her knee or stroking her hand, he was brushing her hair away from her face or playing footsies.

What had Vic told Bobby, anyway? That she was an easy mark?

She had a hard time believing that. Granted, she didn't know Vic very well. He'd let her see only some very carefully chosen aspects of himself. But he sure didn't seem like the kind who would kiss and tell.

Then again, maybe all guys blabbed when they scored. What did she know?

"So, Angela," Bobby said, "it's getting late. You gonna invite me back to your place?"

Angela was appalled. She hadn't given Bobby a single ounce of encouragement, had in fact been dodging his fast hands all evening and deftly turning the conversation away from provocative topics.

She smiled. "No, that won't be a happening thing, not in this lifetime."

"Angela! I'm wounded!"

"You'll get over it," she said dryly. "By tomorrow you will have forgotten all about me, and you'll move on to some new potential conquest." She drained the last of her cappuccino and chucked the empty cup into a nearby trash can.

"I take it that means you don't want to go out again?" He flashed puppy dog eyes at her. Okay, so he was kinda cute, but definitely not her type. Not a guy that made her blood sing through her veins and stole all the air out of her lungs just by looking at her.

Not Vic.

Vic was going to be the measuring stick to which

she applied all future dates for a very long time to come.

When she got home, Angela realized she hadn't even asked Bobby about Vic's phone number. She tried to tell herself she was better off without him. Any relationship that had started off at such a high level of deceit was bound to be doomed. But her sensible, logical statements did little to ease the ache of loneliness that gripped her during the night.

Funny, but she'd never thought of herself as lonely before now.

"YOU DID *WHAT?*" Vic bellowed at his partner the next day as they cruised around their usual beat, a very rough neighborhood in south Dallas. Fortunately, not much was happening on this warm spring Saturday.

Bobby remained unfazed by his partner's rare show of temper. "I took Angela out for coffee. Nice girl, but a cold fish if you ask me. I'm tellin' ya, I was dripping charm, oozing animal magnetism, and she turned up her nose. Take my advice, forget about her. You'd never get to first base with that one."

Vic's initial rage was quickly tempered by the pleasing knowledge that his partner, a guy who seldom heard the word *no,* had struck out with Angela.

"So, you want to stop at Little Angus for lunch?" Bobby asked, the subject of Angela closed and forgotten.

No. He wanted to pound his partner for doing such a lousy job of running interference for him. Then he wanted to call Angela and see if she'd mellowed any. But he suffered through a sliced beef sandwich and endless talk about the Rangers' chances this season, biding his time until he was off the clock.

As it turned out, there was a message waiting for him at the station when he got back from patrol. Angela had called him. He didn't even change clothes first. He went right to the pay phones, Bobby Ray dogging his steps.

"*She* called *you?*" Bobby asked for the third time. "After she turned me down? Me, Bobby 'The Man' Ray? No offense, Steadman, but maybe she has an ulterior motive."

Vic made some impolite references to Bobby's lineage, then threatened to relocate kneecaps if he didn't go away.

"Hello, Angela? Yeah, it's me, Vic." He could hear his own heart pounding in his ears. This was nuts. When was the last time a woman had made him feel like this? He couldn't remember if it had ever happened. Maybe his memories of Kimberly Rose Mundy were fading, but not even his college flame had brought him to his knees the way Angela did.

"Hi, Vic." Just the sound of her voice did crazy things to his nervous system. It conjured up in his imagination everything about her—the softness of her hair, the way she smelled, the little noises she made when she was in the throes of passion.

"I'm glad you called," he said, feeling just like a nerdy teenager who'd finally gotten the prom queen on the phone, then didn't know what to do with her.

"Yeah, me too. I mean…oh, nuts, what *do* I mean?" She laughed nervously.

He liked that. "Do you mean you no longer want to throw things at me?"

"Well, not hard things, anyway. Just pillows, maybe, or really, really ripe tomatoes. Nothing that would leave bruises."

So he wasn't completely off the hook. But this was definitely moving in the right direction.

"Phoebe explained things to me," she went on. "About how you were standing in for your injured partner. I'm truly mortified that my best friends thought my love life was in such sad shape that it called for intervention."

"I'm sure they just wanted you to be happy."

"Yeah, well, they can take their good intentions and stuff 'em. I mean, Bobby Ray? Do you actually spend eight hours a day in a car with that walking bag of hormones?"

Vic laughed. "I'm a guy. He doesn't come on to me."

"I guess that would make a difference," she agreed.

An awkward silence stretched between them. Vic's brain felt paralyzed. This was his chance to make amends, and he was blowing it!

Angela spoke first. "Well, anyway," she said briskly, "I just wanted to let you know that I'm not mad anymore. Not a lot mad, anyway."

Vic wasn't about to let her hang up. "How about—"

"For the record, I don't blame you," she continued. "You were just trying to be chivalrous."

Oh, yeah. Now she was being generous. Maybe he'd started out wanting to protect her, but the predator in him had quickly taken over. "You like hockey?" he asked impulsively. "I have some Stars tickets for tomorrow night."

"Um, yeah. I love hockey."

"Great. Can you be ready by six-thirty?"

"I'll make a point to."

They said their goodbyes and Vic hung up, wondering where he could hustle up a couple of Stars tickets on short notice. He hoped the game wasn't sold out.

SUNDAY AFTERNOON, Angela went through another round of trying everything on in her closet before she settled on a pair of jeans with a wide belt, a plain white shirt and clunky-heeled clogs. Nothing provocative, not much makeup and no perfume. She might be a little naive when it came to men, but she didn't usually make the same mistake twice.

Slow and steady, that was her new motto. No impulse decisions. She would give Vic another chance, but he was going to have to prove to her he liked something about her besides her body.

Unlike their previous date, this time he was early. He didn't slip past the security door this time, either.

Angela resisted the urge to run to the intercom when he rang the bell, forcing herself to walk sedately, let him wait a few anxious moments before she buzzed him in. Her heart beat wildly, all out of proportion to the situation, as she listened to his foot treads growing more distinct as he approached her door.

She flung the door open before he even knocked. So much for slow and steady.

In a tuxedo, Vic had seemed dark and dangerous, but in faded jeans and a soft, hunter-green polo shirt, he was in his element—comfortable and sexy as hell. Just the sight of him whisked all her good intentions away, right along with her breath.

She must have said something that sounded normal, because he smiled and said something back. She couldn't for the life of her remember what.

"Want something to drink before we go?" she asked as her wits gradually returned.

"We better get going. Parking is always terrible down at Reunion."

"Okay." She grabbed her purse and her keys, realizing as she did that something was bothering her. Something about Vic.

As they emerged into the fine spring night, Vic pressed a button on his key chain and a car parked at the curb chirped back.

A car. Silver, SUV, nice. Safe. Not a motorcycle.

He opened her door, then slid behind the wheel and fastened his seat belt.

"Where's your bike?" she asked casually.

"It's supposed to rain. Anyway, I thought you'd be more comfortable in a car."

She remained quiet as Vic pulled away from the

curb and into traffic. Now she knew what was bothering her. This was not the same man who had whisked her off into the night on a motorcycle. This wasn't the same man who'd bowled her over with a rooftop dinner and a fantasy seduction. This wasn't a man who left a woman with no choice but to succumb and enjoy it.

He offered her a piece of gum, which she declined. He asked her about her job and the clinic, and she found herself perfectly at ease, telling him about her two years in nursing school, her sudden decision to change vocations, and how she'd come to work at the funky Be Well Clinic. He told a couple of Bobby Ray stories, which had her laughing despite herself.

He made no attempts to sweep her off her feet.

So what was going on, she wondered?

Vic followed the parking attendant's directions to his designated spot and cut the engine. "We have time to grab a drink before the game, if you want. There's a little bar right across the street."

Angela studied him, his friendly, open, earnest expression, and didn't know whether to laugh with relief or burst into tears. "Okay," she finally said, "who are you and what did you do with Vic?"

Chapter Six

Vic could almost feel himself closing down. He'd thought his evening with Angela was going pretty well, but apparently he'd been overly optimistic.

So Angela wanted the dangerous dude. That was something of a problem, because the man who'd whisked into Angela's life like a tornado, brushing aside her preferences, wooing her with an overwhelming passion she couldn't deny—wasn't him. Oh, sure, it was some aspect of him. But, as much fun as he'd had with the fantasy, the strain of keeping up the facade was too much.

"You mean the overbearing one, the one who led with his libido?" he asked.

Angela smiled. "It hasn't escaped my attention that you've undergone a slight personality adjustment."

He shrugged, uncomfortable. "The other night I put on a show for you."

"So it seems. Why?"

Ah, hell. He wasn't going to dodge this bullet. "Your friends ordered up a fantasy for you. At first I had no intention of playing their little game. Believe me, I'm not into games. But when I saw you...my evil twin just sorta took over.''

"Mmm."

"Like I said before, I wanted you the minute I saw you. Hormones rule. Men are evolutionarily predisposed to do whatever it takes to win over a mate, you know."

Oh, God, what had made him say that? Now she would think he was a calculating, sex-crazed, conscienceless animal. Kind of like Bobby Ray.

To his relief, she laughed.

"What?"

"I was just trying to picture Evil Vic using a word like 'evolutionarily.' I'm not even sure it is a word."

This was his worst nightmare, come to life. He gets a date with the prom queen, and instead of acting cool, he tries to impress her with his intellect. Big mistake. Women never went for brains over brawn.

"So, you, like, really dig Evil Vic," he said, reverting to the persona that apparently turned her on.

"He's intriguing. But the real you isn't something to sneeze at, either. I just don't understand why you felt the need to perpetrate a hoax."

"Oh, come on, Angela. If I'd been Mr. Nice Guy Policeman, you'd never have looked at me twice."

"That's not true. I..." Her voice trailed off as she got a pensive look on her face.

"I'm right, aren't I?"

"I don't know. Evil Vic did push a few buttons that nice men don't normally push. I...I wouldn't have shed my clothes on a rooftop for just any nice guy, no matter how good-looking.''

"Exactly my point. I plead lust-induced insanity and beg for the court's mercy.''

"Hmm, the jury's still out.'' She gave him a mischievous, sideways look, then opened her door.

Vic followed her lead, taking comfort in the fact that he was still in the running. At least she hadn't lunged for the nearest pay phone and called a cab to take her home.

It was another near-perfect spring night, clear and breezy with just a hint of cool in the air. Vic and Angela walked along the sidewalk in companionable silence toward the Reunion Arena entrance, along with dozens of other hockey fans. Vic would have given his motorcycle to know what she was thinking.

Finally she let him know. "So has Evil Vic gone away, now that you've slaked your lust?''

Did she think one night would satisfy him? If anything, he craved making love with her more than he had on that rooftop. Now that he'd had a taste of her sweetness, now that he had memories to savor, he wanted her with a keenness he'd never experienced.

But he'd already made so many missteps with Angela. How to put it?

"Look, Angela.'' He took her arm and guided her to the doorway of a closed deli, out of the stream of foot traffic. "That pushy guy who turned you on was a lot of fun—good for a one-night stand, a steamy affair, maybe. But could you stand to have him walk through your front door night after night, making all the decisions, always getting his way? Is he the kind of guy you want to take home to meet your family? Would you trust him with your sister?''

She narrowed her eyes. ''Don't you go near my sister.''

''That's what I thought.'' He took her hand. ''I don't want just a few nights with you. I don't want some hot, passionate thing if it's just going to burn bright, then burn out. I think you and I…'' He'd said too much already. He couldn't tell, from the ambiguous expression on her face, whether she understood, or if he'd completely alienated her.

She squeezed his hand. ''Okay. Then let's start fresh. We'll forget about all that stuff on the roof.''

Forget the craziest, most exciting sexual episode of his life? Not likely. Angela just wasn't experienced enough to know how incredible their coupling had been.

But at least she wasn't asking him to take her home. At least she was giving him a chance. And that was his goal, right? Later he'd figure out how to rekindle a few rooftop memories.

ANGELA TRIED TO PRETEND she and Vic were out on a first date. In truth, he was exactly the kind of man she'd told her friends she wanted—kind, gentle, polite, good self-confidence, intelligent, gainfully employed. The kind she'd been keeping an eye out for, but had never found.

He was, in fact, a lot like her in some ways. They ought to be able to carry on a civilized, sensible courtship. Angela had always been cautious with relationships, the few she'd had.

But there was something about Vic. The man who'd orchestrated such a powerful seduction wasn't a figment of her imagination. He was there, lurking behind those intense blue eyes. He was part of the man who sat next to her now, munching popcorn and yelling like crazy whenever the Stars even came close to scoring a goal. It fascinated and frightened her at the same time.

Maybe that dangerous, unpredictable vein was the missing element from her previous relationships. Maybe the hint of carefully leashed power was what she'd been craving while going out with all those safe accountants, marketing managers and computer programmers.

The Stars lost by one goal, but it didn't put Vic in a grumpy mood. Another point in his favor. She couldn't stand a guy who got angry over a silly game.

"You want to grab something to eat?" he asked as they moved with the crowd out of the building.

"Eat? I did nothing but eat through the whole game! Nachos, popcorn, chocolate—"

"That doesn't count as dinner."

"I take it you're hungry."

"Starving."

"Don't tell me. You're one of those people with a fast metabolism who can eat anything and everything and never gain weight."

"Okay, I won't tell you. How about coffee, then?"

"I could make coffee at my place." Angela wanted

to bite her tongue as soon as the words were out. They were supposed to be starting fresh, starting slowly, and she'd just invited him into her apartment at...she glanced at her watch. Ten-thirty.

He gave her a searing look as he unlocked the car door. "It might be better if we went out."

Was he thinking the same thing she was? That if they went to her apartment for coffee, kicked their shoes off and got comfortable on the couch, pretty soon the coffee would lose its appeal and they'd be tasting each other instead?

Vic opened the car door for her. "Didn't I see a Starbucks near—"

"No." That was where she and Bobby Ray had gone, and she didn't want her evening with Vic tainted by unpleasant memories. "I mean, yes, you saw one, but I'd rather go to The Cosmic Cup."

Vic smiled. "Oh, yeah. That retro hippie place?"

"Except it's not retro. It's been psychedelic paint and bead curtains since the sixties. My parents used to hang out there when it was new."

"Your parents were hippies?"

"I think they were college kids who wanted to be hippies. They did the long hair and the love beads, but they didn't live in a commune or drop acid."

"Or maybe they just didn't tell you that part."

"You'll have to meet them some time. Trust me, they didn't do acid." Ye gods, she'd just invited him to meet her parents. What was she thinking? That sounded much too serious, when she and Vic barely knew each other.

Except in the biblical sense.

"My parents didn't even pretend to be hippies,"
Vic said. "They were so clean-cut they squeaked.
Then again, neither of them went to college." Vic
puffed out his chest and squinched up his face. "'I
had to work sixty hours a week when I graduated high
school,'" he said, presumably imitating his father.
"'I didn't have time for no sit-ins or love-ins, or
whatever they're called.'"

Angela laughed. "He sounds like a character."

Vic's smile faded. "He was. He died when I was
fourteen."

"Oh, that's sad. How did your family manage?"

He shrugged. "My mom worked. I worked. My
brother worked. We had some life insurance money
and a widow's pension, so we made out okay."

"Where's your mother now?"

He smiled again. "Still living in the same house
where I grew up, in Ennis."

"That's not far from Dallas, is it?"

"Just thirty minutes. I go down to see her most
weekends. She still works full-time at the feed store.
I wish she didn't have to."

Angela could remember hearing somewhere that a
woman should pay attention to how a man treated his
mother, because he would treat his wife the same
way. Now here was a man who loved and respected
his mother. Better still, he wasn't afraid to admit it.
A man secure enough in his masculinity that he didn't
have to constantly flaunt it.

You are in dangerous territory, Angela warned herself. Before long she'd be enshrining Vic and lighting candles to him. Just because she wanted him to be the perfect guy for her didn't mean he was.

They sipped lattes in the funky, cozy interior of The Cosmic Cup. Vic, still hungry, ordered a huge slab of carrot cake, then fed her bites of it despite her protests that she didn't need the calories in that cream-cheese icing. They held hands like a couple of junior-high kids.

But Angela didn't feel as if she was in junior high. Just the touch of his warm hand, innocently brushing hers, sent tingles up her arm and throughout her whole body. Though she kept up her end of the conversation, her mind was crowded with memories of those hands and how they'd felt brushing up against other parts of her.

It was almost midnight by the time Vic drove Angela home. She had every intention of delivering a friendly but chaste good-night kiss at her front door. After all, she had to be at work early the next morning. Anyway, she and Vic were supposed to be starting over.

Every good intention flew right out her ears the moment she looked into those blue eyes, smoky now with desire. Standing on the front porch of her apartment building, he took both her hands in his.

''I had a great time.''

''Me, too.'' She took a deep breath, trying to quell the butterflies in her stomach. It didn't work. ''It's not over yet, is it?'' Angela was stunned those words had come out of her mouth. It was almost as if she'd channeled the provocative question. That wasn't like her. She was normally so careful when it came to men and sex.

"I thought you wanted to take things slow."

"I did. I mean, I do."

"If you invite me inside, I guarantee we aren't going to sit in your living room and play checkers."

Good point, she thought. So, what did she want? A night of mindless passion, or a good night's sleep and a clear conscience, knowing she'd done the reasonable, responsible thing?

No contest. She reached into her purse and pulled out her keys. "I don't even own a checkerboard."

VIC'S BREATH CAUGHT in his chest at what Angela had just said. He'd resigned himself to no more sex with Angela until he'd passed some test, or otherwise proved himself worthy. She'd indicated she wanted a slow, steady courtship, a gradual getting-to-know-you period.

She'd just accelerated the timetable a bit.

"Angela, are you sure?" He couldn't believe he was even asking her that. What guy in his right mind questioned it when a goddess like Angela invited him into her bed?

A guy who didn't want to blow it a second time, he answered himself.

She pushed the door open, stepped inside the dimly lit foyer, then pulled him in after her. "Pretty sure." With that she wound her arms around his neck and planted a kiss on his mouth that made his hair stand on end, not to mention what it did to other parts of his anatomy.

Angela as a timid virgin had been a definite turn-on. But wanton Angela the seductress was mind-blowing. Incapable of giving the matter any more brain power, he scooped her up and headed up the stairs.

She kept kissing him as he made the third-floor landing in record time. She tasted of coffee and cream cheese and something that was all Angela. In his lust-hazed mind, he couldn't even remember which of the six doors along the upstairs hallway was hers.

"Last one on the right," she murmured against his mouth.

He set her down so she could unlock the door, but the moment they were inside her keys and purse dropped with a thud and a clank, and she was in his arms again.

Clothes flew in all directions.

"What about—" he started to ask, but she already knew what he was going to say.

"You left some here the other night," she said with a wicked laugh. "I found them on the floor by the window. They must have fallen out of your pocket when you climbed in. We only used one, remember? So we still have a lo-o-o-ong string of them." She made this speech as she undid his belt and whipped it off, then went to work on his jeans.

He'd created a monster. *Cold fish?* Was that how Bobby Ray had described her? Maybe all those years of repression had caught up with her, and she was making up for lost time.

Whatever the explanation, Vic didn't question it. While she bent over industriously working on his jeans, he unhooked her bra and slid the straps down her arms, freeing her plump, round breasts.

Impatient, he shucked off his own jeans, underwear, socks, then helped her with the rest of her clothing. Every so often they'd take a step toward the bedroom, but by the time they were both naked, they were still only halfway across the living room. What the hell, the couch looked comfortable. Certainly more comfortable than a brick chimney.

He fell back onto the sofa and pulled her with him. She giggled but made no attempt to resist, and instead snugged her body up against his until he was sure no light could pass between them.

This was what he'd missed the first time they'd made love. Having sex while standing up might be exciting and novel, but it involved more logistics and less cuddling than if you just flopped down on a couch.

He liked having Angela all over him. He was blissfully aware of the way her breasts pillowed against his chest, her hard nipples clearly discernible to his sensitized flesh. He liked the way her hair brushed against his neck and shoulders, and how her toes tickled the tops of his feet when she curled and uncurled them.

He could curl her toes. He liked that.

He especially liked the way her soft belly felt

pressed against him, and how if he moved her just so…oh, yes. Now they were getting somewhere.

"Please," she said on a moan.

"Please?" Not "Please stop," he hoped. He would expire right here on her sofa.

"I can't wait any longer."

He was poised at her entrance, so revved up he was about to finish the race before it started, so she didn't have to ask him twice. He plunged inside her warmth, and they sighed together at the rightness of their union.

He'd never felt anything this good. Maybe it was the long buildup of their evening together, or the sudden surprise of Angela's invitation when he'd resigned himself to celibacy. Whatever, it was as if he suddenly had a couple of billion more nerve endings.

"Angela, I can't wait—"

"Neither can I!" She immediately tightened around him and pressed her face against his neck. Her body trembled, and she said his name on an urgent whisper. He couldn't hold back his own satisfaction for one moment longer. He clasped her tightly against him and thrust deeply one final time, and suddenly nothing existed except him and Angela and a moment so perfect he wished he could take a picture of it.

Well, not literally, of course. That wouldn't be one for the family album.

He realized he was holding Angela so tightly he was probably hurting her. He loosened his grip, and she relaxed and slumped against him.

She didn't say anything, and he couldn't think of

any appropriate words himself. He was afraid that if
he opened his mouth, he might say something he'd
regret, something dumb that would spoil the mood.
Like, "Can we do this a couple of times a day for
the rest of our lives?"

As it turned out, though, Angela did her own
mood-spoiling. She lifted her head, looked into his
eyes, and suddenly her own eyes got huge with panic.
"Oh, my God!"

"What? What? Am I hurting you?"

"We forgot to use the—"

"Oh, my God." She was right. They'd talked about
it. But they'd never actually done anything about it.
Vic looked around, hoping maybe he'd see a discarded foil packet, that maybe they'd just forgotten
that they hadn't forgotten. But they'd forgotten, all
right. No wonder he'd thought he'd suddenly grown
new nerve endings. He didn't think he'd ever made
love to a woman without protection. It simply wasn't
something he would consider.

"I'm completely healthy," he reassured her.

She eased away from him and sat up, looking
dazed. "Yeah, me too." But obviously that wasn't
what she was worried about. She grabbed a crocheted
afghan from the back of the sofa and wrapped it
around herself. Whether she was cold or suddenly
self-conscious, he didn't know.

"Jeez, Vic, I don't know what to say."

"'That was great' is always a nice conversation
starter."

She smiled, but it was almost a sad smile. "It was

great. Obviously. So great it put my brain into over-load. Fried it completely.''

"Yeah, me too."

"So what do we do now?"

He sat up and brushed a strand of her hair from her face. "How about we crawl into bed, set the alarm and sleep all wrapped around each other?" It sounded like a plan to him.

"I can't go to sleep!" She sounded horrified that he would even suggest such a thing. "What if I'm... what if I end up..." She couldn't even voice the pos-sibility. She jumped up and started pacing, the afghan wrapped around her like a toga. Except it didn't cover her completely. It had little holes in it, which offered him intriguing glimpses of skin and shadow.

He shook his head to clear it. Right now he had a problem, and jumping Angela's bones again wouldn't solve it. He tried to think logically.

"I can't believe I was so careless!"

"Don't blame yourself," he said, then magnani-mously added, "I was at least half responsible."

"Oh, don't worry, there'll be plenty of blame to spread around if I...if we..."

"If we made a baby," he supplied.

"Don't say it out loud," Angela cautioned. "You might give the powers-that-be ideas."

"Angela, don't wig out on me here."

"I'm allowed to wig out. I've never done anything like this before. I have plans, sensible plans for my life, my career, my retirement. And they don't include having a baby at age twenty-six with no husband!"

Chapter Seven

"Who said anything about no husband? You don't think I'd take responsibility for my own child?"

"Responsibility, yes, I hope so," she said, assuming a more rational tone of voice. "But I wouldn't expect you to marry me, for heaven's sake. Forced marriages aren't necessary in this day and age."

"No kid of mine is gonna get born out of wedlock," he said, knowing he was wigging out a little himself.

"You should have thought of that before you had sex with no protection!"

"Whoa, whoa, wait a minute here. This is getting way out of hand." He stood and went to her, put his arm around her. "Come sit down. Let's talk sensibly about this."

"Yes, you're right." She allowed him to lead her back to the sofa. "We're two intelligent adults, even though we just acted like stupid teenagers. I'm sure we can reach an agreement."

"We don't have to reach an agreement, not tonight."

"But—"

"We won't know if you're pregnant for at least a couple of weeks, right?"

Slowly she nodded.

"There's no sense tearing ourselves up about a baby that might or might not exist. Let's just take a deep breath, and relax." He inhaled, and waited until she followed suit with a short, jerky intake of air. He hadn't realized it until now, but she was perilously close to tears.

Some women got emotional after making love. Maybe that was part of it. He hoped so. He hoped the idea of having his baby wasn't so repugnant to her that it brought her to tears.

They exhaled together. He made her breathe with him twice more. It was a technique he'd used several times to calm down shaky witnesses and crime victims, so they could give him a coherent account of what had happened.

When Angela seemed more relaxed, he stood, drew her to her feet and led her to the bedroom, where a single bedside lamp shone invitingly on the pillow-infested bed. If anything, the room was even messier than the last time he'd seen it. The rest of Angela's house was neat as a CPA's tax return, so he couldn't believe the bedroom was always like this. It amused him to think she put herself into a tizzy just finding the right outfit for a hockey game.

He pulled back the covers on her double bed. "Which side do you like to sleep on?"

"The middle. I've never shared before, remember?"

"Right, smarty. Just get in."

She sat down on the mattress, then scooted over to make room for him. She tossed the afghan aside as she pulled up the covers around them. "Are you going to stay all night?"

"Do you want me to?"

She paused. "I guess it's a little late to be sending you home."

It wasn't the most gracious answer she could have supplied, but he'd take it. "What time do you get up?"

"About seven."

"I have to be at work by seven. Do you have an alarm clock?"

"No, I always just wake up when I'm supposed to."

"Oh." Well, he usually woke up before his alarm went off. He'd be dozing lightly, sleeping with Angela for the first time and all. He didn't think it would be a problem.

ANGELA THOUGHT SHE WOULD never go to sleep. She was tense, edgy, and it felt definitely weird having a naked man snuggled up next to her. She'd never shared a bed with anybody before, not even her sister.

She and Vic started out lying on their backs, her head on his shoulder, just like lovers in a soap opera. But he fell asleep almost immediately, and pretty soon he flopped over, snuggled his face against her breasts and threw one arm over her as if he was afraid she'd escape.

She almost wanted to. It was strange, but it was kind of nice, too. She felt safe. Safe with a man who drove her so insane with lust that she lost all of her common sense.

She didn't think she would be able to sleep at all, but after a while she began to relax. She would just catnap, she decided. She couldn't forget to wake Vic at six.

The next thing she knew, bright sunlight poured through her open curtains. She came immediately awake and bolted upright. "Oh, my God." She squinted at the dainty gold watch on her wrist. It couldn't be right. It couldn't. She held it to her ear, then remembered it was quartz and didn't tick.

"Oh, my God." She gave Vic an energetic shove. "Wake up. Wake up! What time is it?"

Vic opened one bleary eye, squinted against the sunlight, then came fully awake. "What time is it?"

Angela grabbed his arm and pulled it out from under the pillow. His watch read the same as hers. "Ten after nine."

"Holy—" He threw back the covers. "Phone. Phone."

"There." Angela pointed to the imitation French Provincial phone sitting on a delicate writing desk in the corner of her bedroom.

Vic made a dive for it, but it started to ring just as he picked it up.

"Don't—!" Angela yelled as he reflexively put the

receiver to his ear. He stopped himself from answering just in time and handed the phone to Angela. "Hello?"

"Angie?" It was Terri, and she sounded worried. "Where are you?"

Technically Angela was only ten minutes late for work, but she was almost always the first one at the office. It was highly unusual for her to be tardy. No wonder Terri was worried.

"I overslept, can you believe it?"

"Your nine-o'clock is waiting."

Helen Sinclair. Neck and back pain, Angela remembered. "I'll be in in thirty minutes. See if she'll go for thirty minutes instead of an hour, give her a price break and we can push everybody else back fifteen minutes till lunch."

"Got it," Terri said.

Angela was keenly aware of the fact that she and Vic were standing in the middle of her bedroom completely naked in bright sunlight. And that Vic was anxiously waiting for her to get off the phone.

"I have to go. See you in a few minutes." She hung up, handed the phone to Vic, then beat a hasty retreat to the bathroom. She was master of the one-minute shower. She left the bathroom door open, then was amazed at her lack of modesty.

Vic was getting off the phone by the time Angela returned to the bedroom, wrapped in a robe, to paw through her closet. "Are you in trouble at work?" she asked.

"No, not exactly. But someone, somewhere, will

make a note that I'm three hours late for my shift. It doesn't look good.''

She grabbed a powder-blue uniform from the closet, then turned to look at him. ''I'm sorry, truly. I'm a light sleeper and I wake up frequently. I've never slept this late in my life.''

''Me, either.''

''I put out a fresh towel for you in the bathroom. You can use my shampoo and soap and deodorant and stuff, if you don't mind smelling somewhat girly.''

He smiled. ''As long as Bobby Ray doesn't get turned on, I'm okay with it.'' He pivoted and went into the bathroom. Soon Angela heard the water running.

She dressed quickly, pulled her hair into a braid, dabbed on a minimum amount of makeup. Vic was dressed by the time she was ready. She grabbed up her keys and purse and they headed out the front door.

Vic halted her frantic movements as she tried to lock her dead bolt. ''Wait, wait.''

''I'm really late.''

''Then thirty seconds won't make that much difference.'' He turned her around to face him. ''This isn't how I wanted to wake up with you.''

''It's been a little awkward,'' she agreed. ''I wanted to make you some coffee, maybe an English muffin....''

''I wanted to make love again.''

The scratchy morning timbre of his voice and the intimacy of his gaze caused a chill to skitter up and down her spine. Damned if he couldn't get her right back into bed with just a look.

Her braid suddenly felt too tight. Her shoes, too. And her bra. She wanted to be naked again, with her hair wild and loose. "That would have been nice," she said, realizing she sounded lame. *Nice?*

"I'll make it up to you." He kissed her gently at the corner of her mouth, so as not to smear her lipstick, then turned and trotted down the stairs with Angela close behind. He walked her to her car, said a quick goodbye and took off.

Angela felt deflated as she drove to work. So this was the morning after. She'd read about them, heard from her friends about how horrible they could be. Not that this had been horrible. Vic had been sweet, if a trifle distracted by their lateness. But she hadn't reckoned on the cold block of lead that had lodged in her chest the moment he'd been out of her sight.

Would she see him again? Would he call her? Had she ever given him her number? She couldn't remember.

Well, she had his work number, she thought as she pulled in to the clinic parking lot. If nothing else, she would call him when she started her period to let him know he could stop worrying. That would be…she tried to remember when she was due. Less than a week, she thought. She fervently hoped he would get in touch with her before then.

Or maybe not. The man was delicious, no doubt about it, but he turned her into a lunatic. She liked her life orderly and predictable. Safe. She needed a partner who would enhance those aspects of her life, not stir the pot so frantically she didn't know which end was up. Wild flights out the door, late for work, weren't her idea of a good time.

Neither were unplanned pregnancies.

Once inside the clinic, she headed straight for her office and called Terri at the front desk to summon Helen Sinclair. She apologized profusely for the delay, and thank goodness Helen was good-natured and understanding.

Angela worked diligently for the rest of the morning. She was finally able to take a lunch break at one, but she hadn't packed a lunch and she didn't have time to go out. Fortunately there were a couple of leftover doughnuts, an apple from yesterday's lunch and half a bag of corn chips that appeared abandoned, so she helped herself.

Phoebe wandered into the kitchen five minutes later for a soft drink and caught Angela wolfing down the uncharacteristically unhealthy lunch. ''What's with you?''

''Nothing.''

''You overslept, you forgot your lunch? That's not like you.''

''I haven't been getting enough sleep lately,'' Angela said, which was true enough. She lay awake nights reliving her rooftop rendezvous. Now she would have another interlude to add to her repertoire of fantasy memories. ''I guess it just caught up with me.''

''Is anything wrong?''

If Angela thought Phoebe was just being nosy, she'd have given her a curt "no" and left it at that. But Phoebe was the mother hen of the office. Everybody brought their problems to her because she loved helping, and she never failed to notice if someone was a little off kilter. Besides, everyone who worked at the clinic was open and honest. It was what made this such a great place to spend eight or ten hours a day.

"If you have to know, it's Vic."

Phoebe smiled. "That's why you overslept? Cool!"

"No, not cool."

"Why, was he a pig this morning?" Her expression turned fierce. "I'll flatten him if he was. I don't care if he *is* a cop."

Angela grinned at the image of bouncy little Phoebe going toe-to-toe with big, strong Vic. "No, he wasn't a pig. It's just that he makes me act crazy. Irresponsible. Not like me at all."

"Oh, is that all?" A big smile spread across Phoebe's face. "You're in love, honey."

"I am not in love."

"Sure you are. When a man makes you act crazy, it's the definitive sign, the litmus test. You can't sleep, you're thinking about him way too much, maybe you're even thinking about a white picket fence—"

"I am not! That's utterly ridiculous." Well, maybe, when Vic had talked about taking responsibility for his baby, she'd let herself think for one second about what kind of husband he would make. But that was all. Anyway, she'd dismissed the idea. She wouldn't tie any man to her for the wrong reasons.

Phoebe bounced up and went to the fridge to get herself a diet Coke, whistling "Here Comes the Bride."

"You stop that!" Angela threw a wadded-up paper towel at her friend. It didn't even faze her.

"We'll see," Phoebe said, popping the top on her can. "Meanwhile, if you need any advice for how to keep him in line, you just come to Aunt Phoebe." She strutted out of the room, a superior smirk on her face.

Angela looked down at her half-eaten doughnut and promptly lost her appetite. In love? She couldn't be, not after two dates. Infatuated, maybe. Obsessed, possibly. But not in love. Love grew between two people who knew each other, who'd spent lots of time together exploring the things they had in common, who'd seen each other at their best and at their worst, weathering the good times and bad.

Falling in love with Vic would be disastrous to the comfortable life she'd built for herself. So it just wasn't going to happen.

BOBBY RAY HAD A NOSE like a bloodhound and the tenacity of a bulldog. Vic hadn't thought Angela's toiletries were all that perfumey, but apparently they were compared to the ones Vic normally used. In the enclosed squad car, with the morning sun shining in, Bobby Ray picked it up.

"You smell kinda girlie."

Vic sniffed the sleeve of his uniform. "Yeah, must be the fabric softener."

Bobby Ray, who was driving, shot him a suspicious sideways look. "Fabric softener, my aunt Fanny. Some woman's been rubbing herself all over you. And you in uniform, too. Shame, shame."

"You should talk. Bobby Ray Allen, king of the nooner."

"Yeah, well, at least my conquests don't make me late for work."

"I told you, I overslept. My alarm clock didn't go off."

"Right. So who is it? I noticed Marsha Raez didn't come into work today."

"Marsha Raez is married."

"So?"

Good point, Vic thought, if you were Bobby Ray. He never let a wedding ring stop him. One of these days, an irate husband was going to put an end to Bobby's escapades.

"Pull in to that Jack in the Box," Vic said. "I need something to drink. Did you watch the Stars game last night?"

"No, no, no, you're not distracting me. I wanta know who you're getting it from."

A call came over the radio then, requesting assistance at a robbery from all nearby units, which fortunately included Vic and Bobby Ray. They were only blocks away from the crime. Bobby pulled smoothly out of the fast-food line, turned on the lights and siren, and they were off.

One thing about Bobby: he was a damn good cop, especially for a rookie, and Vic couldn't think of anyone he'd rather be sitting next to in a car when the heat was on. In this instance, Vic had never been so grateful for an urgent call.

He scanned the landscape as they headed for the convenience store that had just been robbed. As luck would have it, he caught sight of a man running down a street and ducking into an alley.

"There!" He pointed. Bobby Ray turned down the street, then the alley, where the man Vic had just seen was running even faster. He turned, saw the police car behind him and ducked into a driveway. When the car caught up with him, the suspect was scaling a six-foot privacy fence.

Vic and Bobby leapt out of the car. "Police, freeze!" they yelled in unison as they took up the pursuit on foot. Their warning didn't faze the man. He disappeared on the other side of the fence. Vic cursed under his breath and took a running leap at the fence. Bobby Ray, wiry and agile as a monkey, was over ahead of him, but not by much.

"No guns," Vic said as they chased the man through the yard and out an open front gate. "Not unless he draws on us." Vic believed they could wear him out. He'd been running longer than them.

They pursued him across a street and over a chain-link fence, where he slowed down when his sleeve caught on a barb. He tore loose and kept running, but by then Vic and Bobby were only a few feet behind him.

"Stop!" Vic tried again. "We've got you now. Stop." He vaulted over the fence, cutting the hell out of his hand in the process. But the man was cornered. High bushes surrounded the fence on all the remaining escape routes. He hesitated, and that was just enough time for Vic to tackle him to the ground.

Working like a couple of rodeo bulldoggers, Vic and Bobby had the suspect on his face and cuffed in no time flat. Without even touching the bag he'd been holding, they could see it contained wads of cash.

Bingo.

Vic spoke a few words into his portable, summoning backup. He instructed Bobby Ray to stay with the suspect, then he headed back to the car to find something to bandage his hand with. He was bleeding all over his uniform.

At least, he thought wryly, he'd done something good. He'd get a gold star in the same file where they kept a record of his being late to work. Maybe the two would offset each other.

When he got back to the car, he found that his shift commander, Lieutenant Richard Gage, had pulled up behind him and was scowling at the car's open doors and flashing lights. Without saying a word, he walked over to the driver's side, reached in and jerked out the keys.

"Were you driving this car, Steadman?"

Vic gulped. Leaving your keys in your patrol car was a dumb, dumb thing to do. But this was Bobby Ray's first foot chase, and he'd lost his head a little bit.

Vic decided not to get Bobby in trouble. Bobby was still in his probationary period, during which he could be dismissed with virtually no cause.

"The perp was getting away," he said in his own defense, trying to fudge the issue without any outright lies. "I guess we were in a hurry."

Gage narrowed his eyes. "Wait a minute. Don't tell me. You weren't driving. It was your partner!"

"He got excited," Vic said. "I should have paid more attention."

"Don't try and stick up for him. When an officer, no matter how green, is driving this car, he's responsible for it."

"Yes, sir. We caught the robber."

"And your car could have been stolen in the meantime. A couple of hundred dollars cash versus a thirty-thousand-dollar automobile. Think about it."

Well, Vic thought, so much for his delusions of heroism.

"From now on I want you driving, not that screw-up rookie. At least for a while."

"Yes, sir." Personally, Vic thought the best way for Bobby Ray to learn was to drive, but now probably wasn't the time to speak his mind.

Bobby Ray came up behind him, the suspect in tow. He must have heard the last part of Gage's harangue, because he gave Vic a look that said, *Thanks for trying.*

"You're bleeding," Gage said to Vic, almost accusingly.

"Yes, sir."

"Better have that stitched up."

"I'm sure it's not—" He stopped. The way the lieutenant was looking at him, he dared not argue. "Yes, sir."

It was mid-afternoon by the time Vic got out of the emergency room. He hadn't eaten all day, his hand was throbbing from the cut and the eight stitches, his muscles ached from the chase. In short, he was a mess.

Bobby Ray picked him up and drove him back to the station. He was uncharacteristically quiet.

"Something wrong?" Vic asked.

Bobby Ray took a deep breath. "I left the keys in the ignition."

"We all make mistakes. It was your first foot chase. You were caught up in the excitement. Just don't do it again."

"You tried to take the heat for me."

"And got us both in hot water instead."

"I still appreciate it. I'll return the favor some day." A short pause. "So, who's the babe you're doing?"

Vic almost snarled. "You can do me a favor by shutting up. I don't want to talk about it."

"Oh, my God, don't tell me it's the fish."

Vic felt his muscles tensing, his jaw clenching.

"It is! I can tell by the look on your face. I don't get it. How come she's putting out for you and not me?"

"Bobby Ray, if you don't shut up, I'm going to knock out all your pretty white teeth."

Chapter Eight

Vic went home and anesthetized himself with beer and bad cable movies. He wanted to call Angela, but he didn't figure he'd be very good company. Besides, he had to rethink this Angela thing.

Enjoying a woman's company was one thing. But when that enjoyment interfered with his job, that was another. He'd shown up for work late and smelling like a flower shop, if Bobby Ray could be trusted. He hadn't been getting enough sleep because of Angela, and a sleep-deprived cop was a menace to society and a danger to his partner.

In his zeal to perform today, he'd taken risks with his squad car, carelessly injured himself and set a bad example for the rookie he was supposed to be training. Yeah, he'd caught the bad guy, but the ends didn't always justify the means.

He decided to wait a day or two and give both himself and Angela time to wind down. Besides, he *still* didn't know her phone number.

BY FRIDAY ANGELA WAS a basket case. She hadn't
heard a peep from Vic, and she was a day late. Not
that her monthly cycles operated on a precise schedule, but she was early as often as she was late. Why
couldn't she be early this month?

She called in sick. She just couldn't do justice to
her clients when she was so distracted. She opened a
box of caramel popcorn she'd been saving for a special occasion, turned on the TV and ate breakfast
watching old sitcoms.

By noon she'd eaten every fattening, unhealthy
thing she could find in her pantry, fridge and freezer.
Were these pregnancy cravings? she suddenly wondered. Or just PMS?

Just after noon the doorbell rang. Angela immediately panicked. What if it was Vic? She was wearing
Scooby Doo pajamas! Still, her curiosity got the best
of her. She went to the intercom. "Yes?"

"Angie, it's me, open up." Phoebe.

Angela felt both relieved and disappointed as she
buzzed her friend into the building. She hadn't
wanted Vic to see her in this pathetic state, but, oh,
how she wanted to see him.

Phoebe, bless her, had brought lunch in the form
of two submarine sandwiches, potato salad and
soda—real soda, not diet.

"I am so worried about you," Phoebe said as she
barged in. "You never call in sick. The stud's not
here, is he?"

"No, more's the pity." If she was going to take a
personal day off from work, wouldn't it have been

nicer to loll around in bed with Vic instead of indulging in this ridiculous pity party?

"So, are you really sick?" Phoebe asked as she moved into the kitchen and started setting the table. Angela knew she shouldn't have been hungry, but she was.

"Sick at heart." And before she knew it she was pouring out the whole mortifying story to Phoebe, about how she forgot the condoms and now she was afraid she was pregnant and she was afraid Vic was tired of her already because he hadn't called.

"Oh, you poor thing," Phoebe said, then added, "Welcome to the club."

"What club?"

"RCW. Romantically Challenged Women. We whine incessantly about how there are no good men, and then when we find one, we make ourselves miserable obsessing about him and do stupid things."

Angela had to admit that was the pattern her friends generally followed, behavior she'd previously found very silly.

"Okay," Phoebe said, getting practical as she cleared away the debris from lunch. "Worst-case scenario?"

That was easy. "I'm pregnant, and Vic wants nothing to do with me."

"Do you think that will happen? Really?"

Angela thought hard. "No. When he realized what we did the other night, he immediately wanted to take responsibility. The real worst-case scenario is that he *would* take responsibility, but he would resent me and the kid for the rest of our lives.''

"That's grim," Phoebe agreed. "Okay. Best-case scenario?"

This was also an easy question. "We fall in love and get married because we want to, not because there's a baby."

"Ah-hah!"

"Ah-hah, what?" What had she said? Angela wondered.

"Most women would have said the best-case scenario is that they're not pregnant. You didn't even think of that. Ergo, you *want* to be pregnant. You want to have Vic's child, so you subconsciously forgot the condoms on purpose."

Angela just sat there, stunned. First Phoebe had concluded Angela was in love. Now she'd decided Angela had purposely gotten pregnant.

What if she was right...on both counts?

IT HAD BEEN PMS AFTER ALL. Angela knew she should have been overwhelmingly relieved. She should have thanked God, the fates and maybe Buddha and Siva just to be on the safe side, then she should have vowed she would never, ever, do anything that stupid again.

In fact, she did all those things. But she was also disappointed.

Only now did she let herself think about what kind of father Vic would have been. Kind, caring, involved? Or remote, distant, financially responsible but absent? She wanted to believe the former. She could almost see him dandling a baby boy on his knee or helping a little girl with her math homework. But truthfully, she just didn't know him well enough to confidently cast him in the role of family man.

She ought to call him, she decided. She tried the police station first, but he wasn't on duty. On a whim she asked for Bobby Ray, but he wasn't available, of course. He called her back a couple of hours later.

"So, you changed your mind about me?"

That put her on the defensive. "I, um, well—"

He laughed. "Just kidding. I'm a graceful loser, I promise. This is probably about Vic."

He had her there. "Yeah. I need his home number. I, um, lost it. It's important."

"Okay, but you're destroying my self-esteem. Vic's a nice guy, but I could have showed you a better time."

She didn't think he was serious. Surely Bobby Ray wouldn't try to steal a woman his partner was seeing, even if said partner had made no claims to said woman.

Bobby gave her the number. "I'm sure he'll enjoy hearing from you," he said, sounding serious for a change. "He's really moping around with that mandatory leave."

"Mandatory leave!" Angela repeated with alarm. Had he gotten in real trouble over his tardiness the other day? She knew the police department was big on discipline, and that Vic's captain was a real stickler, but—

"Yeah, you know, for the hand. Okay, well, I gotta go. Treat my partner good, now." He hung up before Angela could ask what he meant about Vic's hand.

She immediately dialed Vic's number, relieved beyond measure that he answered right away.

"It's Angela. I'm not pregnant, so you can stop avoiding me, and what's wrong with your hand?"

"Hello to you, too." His voice was warm, welcoming, but it held a note of tension as well. "Are you at home?"

"Yes, but—"

"I'll be over in half an hour. And I haven't been avoiding you."

Oh, great, she thought as she hung up. It would take her half an hour to get her apartment straightened up. Then what about herself? She decided her personal hygiene took priority. Vic would just have to live with her housekeeping weaknesses. Although, come to think of it, she was normally a perfect housekeeper. How had she let things get so out of control?

Thirty minutes later—on the nose—Vic rang the doorbell. Angela buzzed him in, then checked herself in the hall mirror one more time. Faded jeans, a casual knit top with little flowers on it, her hair in a hasty twist with a clip. She didn't bother with shoes, and she wore no makeup except for a bit of mascara and some clear lip gloss. It would have to do.

She opened the door just as he was tapping on it, and Angela didn't know where to look first—at the bouquet of wildflowers in his left hand, the swath of bandages on his right, or the wicked grin on his handsome face. All three did something to her heart.

"Why flowers?" she blurted out.

"For having to worry about being pregnant in the first place," he said. "I can't imagine it was much fun, and I'm sorry I was so irresponsible that I let it happen."

She took the flowers, sniffed them appreciatively. "Thank you. What happened to your hand?"

She led him inside and he closed the door behind him. "An unfortunate altercation with a chain-link fence."

"Now, *that* doesn't sound pleasant. Come into the kitchen so I can find a vase for the flowers."

He followed her, offering no further explanation.

"So, how did it happen?" she asked as she searched through her kitchen cupboards for her good vase. Her hand ached just looking at those bandages. "What were you doing wrestling a fence?"

"Jumping over it. Chasing a convenience-store robber."

Angela gasped. She stopped looking for a vase and turned to face him. "Oh, my God. Did you catch him?"

She thought his chest puffed out just a bit. "Yeah, I did."

"Do you chase bad guys very often?" She hadn't given a whole lot of thought to exactly what he did on the job. Theoretically she knew cops put themselves in danger, but she also knew it wasn't like TV. The only specifics he had mentioned involved amusing Bobby Ray anecdotes. She knew Vic patrolled a not-so-great neighborhood, and that he answered calls about thefts and suspicious persons and stolen vehicles, but...

"Not very often. It was Bobby Ray's first time. Is this what you're looking for?" He pointed to a cut-crystal vase sitting on her breakfast table, filled with silk flowers.

"Oh, yeah, thanks." She pulled out the silks, unwrapped the wildflowers, put them in the vase and filled the vase with water. When she was finished she set it back on the table. All the while she was acutely aware of Vic's overwhelming presence in her tiny kitchen. He made her feel as if she was living in a dollhouse. She thought again about redecorating in more solid furniture, brighter colors, simpler lines. She wanted her apartment to be someplace where Vic felt at home.

"Bobby Ray mentioned you're on leave," Angela said as they went into the living room. She sat down in a chair, not daring to sit next to him on the sofa. She was too fragile right now, too vulnerable. One look, one touch, and she'd be all over him like white on rice.

"Just till Monday," he said. "Then it's a desk job until the hand heals."

"How long will that be?"

"Probably a couple of weeks." He sighed. "A couple of weeks in prison."

"You don't like desk work, I take it."

"Hate it. I like to be outside. I used to do bicycle

patrol, but my knee started bothering me, so I had to quit.''

''Old football injury?''

''Skiing.''

''I love to ski!''

''Me, too. Can't do it anymore, though.''

''Oh.'' Angela was disappointed. She thought about the two of them taking romantic weekends to Taos or Copper Mountain, flying down the slopes together, cozying up in front of a fireplace in the evenings….

''So, you want to go out somewhere?'' Angela asked. ''We could go to the park. You don't have a dog, do you? Because whenever I go to the park, I see all these people playing with their dogs and I think how much fun it would be….'' She was babbling.

''No, no dog. I like dogs, though.''

''Yeah, me too. We could go to the humane society and adopt one.'' Good heavens, what was she saying? To suggest joint ownership of a dog was almost as bad as offering to have his child! Anyway, she couldn't own a dog. Her apartment building allowed small pets, but she couldn't take on that responsibility. She was gone too much. It wouldn't be fair.

It still sounded like a fun idea.

Vic smiled at her enthusiasm. ''I don't think that would be very practical.''

''No, me neither. I get the craziest notions when I'm around you. I don't understand it.''

''I *do* the craziest things when I'm around you.''

So why was he sitting all the way across the room, practically, when she'd prefer it if he'd do something crazy, like kiss her? Maybe if they made love right now, they could get it over with, stop being so edgy and enjoy the rest of the afternoon.

"I'm not normally an impulsive person," Vic continued.

"Me, neither." Without really thinking about it, she got up and joined him on the couch. "Could you just hold my hand or something? I'm feeling really weird." She held out her hand, palm up, the way she might befriend a nervous animal.

Vic jumped up from the couch. "No touching. I mean, I think touching is a bad idea."

Angela stared at him, surprised. "You didn't think it was a bad idea the other night."

"Things have changed."

Uh-oh. This sounded unencouraging. She had a sneaking suspicion she was about to get dumped, and the relationship hadn't even started.

She decided to go on the offensive. "If you wanted to stop seeing me, all you had to do was give me a polite kiss-off over the phone."

"Angela, it's not like that." He sat back down, and he did take her hand. "I'm crazy about you. You don't deserve to be broken up with over the phone."

"So you came over to do it in person?" Now she was the one who jumped up, jerking her hand out of his light grasp. "Did you think the flowers would make it easier? Well, don't do me any favors. It would have been much better over the phone. That way I could have just hung up, and you wouldn't see me…'' She was horrified that her eyes were filling up with tears. This was sheer humiliation. She turned away from him.

He came up behind her, put his hands on her shoulders. ''Angela, please, don't cry. Could I just explain?''

''Yeah, fine, whatever.'' She wiped her eyes with the back of her hand, glad she hadn't finished her makeup. At least she wouldn't have raccoon eyes.

''It's me, not you.''

''Oh, please. That is such a cliché.''

''I was almost three hours late for work Monday. I am never late. I'm a by-the-book kind of guy. Did you know cops all have nicknames?''

She frowned at the seeming non sequitur. ''No.''

''Well, they do. You know what mine is?''

''No.''

''Steady Steadman. Until recently, that is. Now it's 'Romeo.' That's not exactly the sort of reputation I want to cultivate.''

She couldn't blame him there. Her friends' teasing about her love life had bothered her, too.

''I have never been late for work since I joined the police department.''

''It was one lapse,'' she pointed out, sniffing back the humiliating tears. ''Cut yourself some slack.''

''It's not just that I was late. I was also tired because I didn't get enough sleep. I'm supposed to be supervising Bobby Ray, and instead I made some terrible decisions that resulted in my shift commander yelling at me for five solid minutes while I bled all over my uniform. I've never done that before, either. I had a spotless record.''

Angela's urge to weep receded as she realized what Vic was saying. She had disrupted his life in the same way he'd disrupted hers. Apparently he was more like her than she'd realized. They were both used to being in complete control of their lives, taking pride in their responsibility and reliability. Suddenly becoming preoccupied with a lover had fouled up his routine and altered his judgment, just as it had hers.

"Oddly enough, I understand," she said.

"I've never had unprotected sex before. Never."

"So what you're saying is that I'm wrecking your life."

"I'm wrecking my own life, but it's because I'm so nuts about you."

"I could say the exact same thing."

"I did something similar in college. I had a four point zero GPA until I met this girl, and then I just let everything slide—well, never mind. That's not important." He was talking very fast now, letting the words pour out as he kept hold of her shoulders. "If it were any other time, I might be able to handle it. But I'm up for a promotion to sergeant and I've put in a request for a detective slot that's opening up in the burglary unit. The brass is watching me really carefully right now. If I screw up, I might wind up a uniform the rest of my life."

"Is…is a detective's job safer than a patrolman's?" she asked.

"What? Um, yeah, generally speaking. What does that have to do with anything?"

"Just that I hadn't realized how dangerous your job was. I'd like for you to get that detective's job."

"Then my performance has to be impeccable. I have to put a hundred percent of my concentration into my job."

"Which means you don't have time for a relationship."

"Not right now. Maybe when I get my career nailed down…"

"Oh, that'll be fine. I'll just sit around and wait for six months, or a year, or two years…however long it takes."

"You want to wait?"

She pulled away from him and whirled around to face him. "That was sarcasm, Vic. Look, I've been thinking along the exact same lines as you. My life was even and predictable till you came along. In the past week I've been late to work, skipped my exercise routine, eaten enough junk food to sink the Queen Mary and thought I was pregnant. Fun as it's been, I'm not sure this relationship is healthy for either of us."

Vic looked surprised. "So you think we should stop seeing each other, too?"

She took a deep breath. *No!* her mind screamed. "Yes. Oh, what's the matter? That's what you want me to say, right?"

"No. I mean, yes, but I was thinking more along the lines of a temporary thing."

Angela shook her head. "It wouldn't be any different six months or a year from now. We just have to face the fact that we're bad for each other, and let it go."

Vic couldn't believe his ears. He'd come here to temporarily break things off with Angela, but when push came to shove he hadn't wanted to irrevocably end the relationship. Now she'd turned the tables on him and broken up with him herself.

Bobby Ray had told him he was crazy to want to dump a "hot number" like Angela, but that if he did break up with her, she would cry and carry on and beg him to stay with her. Well, there'd been a few tears, but certainly no begging.

He knew he should be relieved. He wasn't. How fair was that?

"I'm glad you're being so reasonable," he said. "Would it be all right if I called you in a few months? Maybe things will be different."

Her eyes got steely. "Don't bother. Let's just be thankful we realized the mistake we were making before any real harm was done." She stalked over to the door and opened it. "I'm sure you can find your own way out."

Ouch. That was the other possibility Bobby Ray had warned him about. That she'd be royally ticked off. He'd nailed that one.

"I wish you wouldn't be angry."

"How else should I handle it?" she asked, quite sensibly, he thought. "Do you want me to whine and beg you to change your mind? I didn't think you had that kind of ego.''

"I guess I just didn't expect you to agree with me so quickly.'' And yeah, it did sting his ego.

"Would you prefer me to smile and act like it's no big deal? Well, it is a big deal, damn it. Oh, and that's another thing. I never cursed until I met you.''

"Baloney. You were cursing at your car that first night I met you.'' His heart ached just remembering how forlorn she'd been, how instantly attracted he'd been. "Anyway, if it's such a big deal, how come you agreed to it so quickly?''

"Because it's the right thing to do. Not because it doesn't hurt. Just let me hold on to my anger, okay? It's easier that way.'' She wasn't making sense, and she wasn't being fair. But her emotions were way out of whack. "Now get out.''

He did. But this hadn't gone at all the way he'd planned.

Vic relived the scene with Angela, and her quick-silver moods, a dozen or more times on the drive home. Each time, the scene ended differently, but it usually involved clothes flying through the air.

He'd done the right thing. He knew it. Then why did he feel so rotten? He tried to think about his promotion and found himself thinking, *big deal.* A new title, a little pay raise. Yeah, that was worth giving up the most intriguing woman he'd ever met, the most mind-blowing sex he'd ever experienced. Right.

Landing the detective's job, though—that was worth just about anything. No more patrolling miserable neighborhoods with Bobby Ray. No more breaking up bar fights, or being the first guy through the door on a drug raid. He would have an office—okay, a cubicle and a desk, probably shared with another detective—and he'd be using his brain instead of his brawn.

Working as a detective was all he'd ever wanted. He couldn't throw that dream away, not even for a woman as wonderful as Angela Capria. He just had to keep telling himself that.

Chapter Nine

Victoria, Terri and Phoebe arrived at the Women's Expo at the crack of dawn to set up the clinic's booth, where they were offering a free "Ask-a-Nurse" service and five-dollar chair massages for charity.

Sarah had to drive her nephew to soccer practice, so she was exempted from the setup. Dr. Nausbaum, the gung-ho organizer of the clinic's participation in this event, was home in bed with a cold, dosing herself with herbal tea.

"So where's Angela?" Terri asked as she and Phoebe set up tables.

"I told her to sleep in. Hope y'all don't mind."

"Not at all. She needs the rest," Victoria piped up. She was up on a ladder hanging their banner on the back wall of the booth. "Angie's looked really awful all week."

"It's that rotten Vic," Terri groused. "Typical man. Gives a girl the full-court press, and just when she's fallen head over heels, he dumps her."

"Oh, I don't think he's so bad." Phoebe said.

"What?" Victoria and Terri said together, staring at her as if she'd grown another head.

"I talked to Bobby Ray. He says Vic's wandering around the station like the walking wounded, with sad puppy-dog eyes. He's as crazy for Angie as she is for him."

The three women gave up any pretext of working. Phoebe perched on the edge of the table while the other two flopped into metal folding chairs.

"I don't get it," Victoria said. "If they're so nuts about one another, why did they break up?"

"My opinion?" Phoebe said. "They're both scared to death. We know Angela's never been involved in a serious relationship. Bobby Ray hasn't known Vic all that long, but he claims Vic's never talked about any past girlfriends. I think this is the first time either one of them has experienced really strong romantic feelings—you know, the kind that make you crazy."

The other women nodded in understanding.

"Angela is a bit of a control freak," Terri said. "I mean that in the nicest way, but she always seems to have her stuff together, you know? Gets her hair trimmed every six weeks—"

"And she's always a month early renewing her car insurance."

"Has the oil changed every three months."

"Saves for retirement."

"Makes lists."

Phoebe nodded vigorously. "Then Vic comes along, and she forgets everything—*everything*—but him."

"We have to do something," Terri said. "Maybe these two are really meant for each other. I mean, it sounds like they have a lot in common."

"Whoa, wait a minute," Victoria said. "Last time we interfered in Angela's love life she almost disowned all of us."

"Not to worry," Phoebe said. "I've already taken care of it."

"What'd you do?" Terri asked.

"The Women's Expo has to have security, right? And who do they recruit for security?"

"Off-duty police officers," Victoria and Terri said together.

"Let's just say I pulled a few strings. And with Bobby Ray's help, it'll all come together."

Victoria and Terri shared conspiratorial smiles with Phoebe. "Phoebs," Victoria said, "you're brilliant. But if Angela asks, I'm denying all knowledge."

Just then Angela came rushing up with her usual array of tote bags containing everything anybody might possibly need. She stopped and stared at the half-put-together booth, then gave the others a curious look that bordered on suspicious. "Y'all have been busy, I see."

Phoebe stood and clapped her hands crisply. "Okay, coffee break's over. Back to work, everybody."

VIC STROLLED THE AISLES of the trade show with Bobby Ray at his side, keeping on the lookout for trouble, though he couldn't imagine what could possibly happen at a Women's Expo, unless it was a riot at the booth where they were giving away free romance novels.

"Why are we doing this again?" he asked Bobby Ray.

"Community service. Looks good on the old résumé."

Vic supposed he could use all the gold stars he could scare up after last week's fiasco. He'd been early to work every day this week, prompt, courteous and altogether Boy Scout-like, hoping to prove to his captain that his tardiness was just a fluke, never to be repeated.

Captain Sikes hadn't seemed to notice. Every day he'd asked how Vic's hand was coming along. That seemed to be the extent of his interest in Vic. Once, Vic had inquired if any progress had been made on the decision as to who would fill the soon-to-be-vacant detective's slot. Sikes had grunted at him and curtly informed him that he'd be the first to know if he got the job, or the promotion.

Vic wasn't encouraged.

"You're really tense lately," Bobby Ray commented. "I've gotten used to the fact that you don't really get my jokes, but now you walk around like a two-by-four and you never crack a smile."

Vic knew he'd been short with Bobby lately. Bobby was partnering with somebody else for the time being, but he never missed an opportunity to hang out by Vic's temporary desk and razz him.

"It's been a tough week," Vic said. "I hate desk work."

"Yeah, well, I think you need to loosen up, and I have just the ticket."

"Not a woman."

"No, no."

"Or a beer?" Technically they were on duty. Though they weren't on the city payroll today, they were in uniform.

"For gosh sake, Steadman, give me some credit. I saw a booth against the wall on the other side of the exhibit hall where you can get a chair massage. Five bucks."

"I didn't bring any money with me today." He didn't want a massage. He liked feeling tense and grumpy. He liked wallowing in self-pity. The more he wallowed, the sooner he'd get over Angela, he reasoned.

"Well, I did. The money goes to an abused women's shelter."

"Not interested."

"Aw, come on. You'd do those poor, abused women out of five bucks?"

"Why don't *you* get a massage?"

"I don't need one like you do."

"We're supposed to be working security, not entertaining ourselves."

"We're allowed coffee breaks. Come on." Bobby Ray took Vic's arm and virtually dragged him toward the other side of the World Trade Center exhibition hall.

Vic gave in. Once Bobby Ray got an idea into his head, it was impossible to dissuade him. Besides, maybe a massage would do him some good. His neck and shoulder muscles had been going into spasms lately, a condition he hadn't suffered since…well, since college. Since his breakup with Kimberly Rose Mundy.

Vic didn't catch on until he and Bobby were right in front of the Be Well Clinic's booth. Duh! Angela was a massage therapist. She was just finishing up a massage on an older woman. Engrossed in her work, she didn't even see Vic.

"Ladies!" Bobby Ray announced. "I have a man here in dire need of a massage, and a crisp, five-dollar bill for the women's shelter."

A pretty, delicate-boned blonde in a nurse's uniform took Vic by the arm while several other attractive young women—all workers at the clinic, apparently—looked on, amused. There would be no graceful escape from this.

"Come right this way, Officer," said the blonde, whose name tag read Victoria. "Experience Angela's magic fingers."

Angela, who had just helped her previous client out of the chair and was shaking hands, glanced over at the sound of her name. She went pale as milk. Her gaze locked with Vic's, and for one heart-stopping moment there were only the two of them in the universe.

He hadn't realized how much he'd missed her till he saw her face-to-face. She looked beautiful. She also looked a little bit tired, though, and purple shadows darkened the area under her eyes.

Had he done that to her?

"Hello, Vic," she murmured, breaking the spell. "Looks like our well-meaning friends are at it again."

"Um, yeah." Vic spared a glance for his partner, whom he was going to kill later. He was huddled with a couple of Angela's friends, whispering conspiratorially. At his hard glare, they suddenly found pressing business elsewhere.

He turned back to Angela. "You don't have to do this if you don't want to."

She tossed her braid over her shoulder. "I don't see why not. I'm a professional. You're just a body to me."

He hoped she was lying. Angela would never, ever, be just a body to him.

"Unless you'd rather not," she said, a challenging gleam in her eye.

"Oh, no, I'm game. I wouldn't dream of worming out of this now. Besides, Bobby's parting with five of his hard-earned dollars for this."

Angela pulled a tissue from a box and placed it on the face rest. "Sit down, then. Turn toward the back of the chair, face resting against the tissue." Her voice was utterly impersonal.

He could do this, Vic told himself. He straddled the odd-looking chair and sat as she directed and pressed his face into the doughnut-shaped face rest.

"Is that comfortable?"

"Yes, fine."

He could do this. This meant nothing to him. She was just a massage therapist, and he couldn't even see her. Her hands could belong to anyone. His mother. His third-grade teacher. Yeah, Mrs. Higdon, the unsexiest woman he'd ever known.

But the second Angela put her hands on him, he was a goner.

ANGELA COULDN'T BELIEVE her friends were playing matchmaker—again! She'd had a feeling they were up to something when she'd seen them huddled together this morning, then jumping apart guiltily just as she'd arrived.

As she kneaded Vic's strong shoulders, she looked around her, ready to beam accusing glances at anybody and everybody in range. But miraculously every one of the conspirators—and she knew they were *all* in on it—had vanished from the booth. It was just her and Vic, and her hands were all over him.

At first, all she could think of was how good he felt. He had all kinds of muscles—deltoids and biceps and triceps—all perfectly delineated. This was a body that worked out regularly. Her face heated at the memory of how those muscles had looked when Vic was naked, when her hands could roam at will over rippling stomach muscles and his firm gluteus maximus.

But then professionalism took over. He was really tight, as in tense. She found a knot in his shoulder and gently worked it with her thumb, earning a sharp intake of breath from Vic.

"Sore?"

"Yeah."

"Sorry, I'll go easier."

"No, just keep doing what you're doing. It hurts good."

Angela continued her massage. She had to endure eight more minutes of this. On the other hand, she had a captive audience. If there was anything she wanted to say to Vic, now was the time.

"So how are you doing?" she asked, trying to sound casual.

"Bored out of my mind. Thank God I get to go back on active duty next week."

That wasn't what she meant, but she'd take it. At least they were having a civil conversation. "Then your hand must be recovering okay."

"Yeah, it hardly hurts at all."

She worked her fingers down his right arm toward the injured hand, which now sported only a small bandage held on with adhesive tape. Careful to avoid the injury itself, she massaged his wrist, his palm, his fingers. A little reflexology might speed up the healing.

"I'm sorry I got so mad at you," she said carefully, working her way down the other arm. "Normally I don't let emotions dictate my behavior."

"Can we just not talk about it?" he said curtly. "Can we just get through this? It wasn't my idea, you know."

"Fine." She moved to his neck, digging in with her thumbs a little deeper than necessary.

"Ow!"

"Well, I was just trying to be civil. You didn't have to bite my head off."

"I don't want to be friendly with you, Angela."

That stung. She came close to dumping him out of the chair, and maybe giving him a swift kick for good measure. But what he said next gave her pause.

"Because if we start getting friendly, we'll be right back in bed. You know it, and I know it. I've been thinking about everything you said, and you were right. Staying mad makes it easier. Better we part enemies."

She rubbed his ears, which was supposed to have a soothing effect. "So sex is the problem?"

"In a nutshell."

"That's what I thought. I've always believed that sex outside of a committed relationship was a bad idea, and I was right. It never should have happened."

"So what *should* have happened?"

"I don't know," she answered impatiently. Now that she'd tasted the forbidden fruit, she had a hard time imagining being with Vic and not going to bed with him. Physical intimacy with him felt as natural as falling off a log. "I certainly don't have all the answers."

He was quiet for a time, except for an occasional sigh of pleasure. Then he asked, "Do you think a relationship without sex can work?"

"It does for some people."

"Is that what you're suggesting?"

She massaged his scalp, losing her fingers in his soft, thick black hair. "I'm not suggesting anything. Anyway, we already tried starting over fresh, and it didn't work."

"Yeah, but we didn't have a no-sex rule. Oh, oh yeah, that's it."

She'd found another tension knot at the base of his skull, so she worked it until it was gone, enduring Vic's encouragement, which sounded suspiciously like sex talk to her. "Sit up," she instructed. He did, giving her access to his cheeks and jaws.

By accident, one of her fingers strayed near his mouth. He licked it. She slid it between his lips, wondering what madness possessed her now. He sucked on it. A soft moan escaped him.

"That rule wouldn't last...oh, my...five minutes," she said.

"It might," he said around her finger. "I have will-power."

"Yes, I can see that." She pulled her hand out of his reach. What had happened to that nice, healthy anger he'd been harboring? This massage had felt a lot safer when he was mad.

"No, really." He pushed himself up off the chair and turned around so he could sit facing her. "This could work."

Angela didn't know what to make of his sudden turnaround. A minute ago he'd claimed he didn't even want to carry on a polite conversation.

"It's ridiculous," she said. "You just can't stand

it that I'm not begging you to come back. So you're going to win me over again, then when your little 'no-sex' plan doesn't work, you'll walk away again. Well, no thanks. Better we part enemies, like you said.''

They stared at each other for a few seconds, challenging, both of them breathing as if they'd just sprinted up and down the aisles of the trade show. Then—and she had no idea how it happened—she was kissing him. She was sitting in his lap plastered to him so that a piece of tissue paper couldn't fit between them, and she was kissing the daylights out of him right there in the middle of the Women's Expo.

Vic came to his senses first, breaking the kiss, for which she was grateful. He wore a really goofy smile, though, as he set her on her feet, then stood up himself.

''Thank you, Ms., um…'' He looked at her badge. ''Ms. Capria,'' he said in a loud voice. ''That really worked the kinks out. I'll recommend your clinic to my friends.'' He strolled out of the booth. It was then Angela realized they had an audience, a group of teenage boys—Lord only knew what they were doing at a Women's Expo. They were all holding five-dollar bills.

''Hey, ma'am, can I have a massage like that?'' one of them asked politely.

''Me, too.''

''Me, three.''

''If you get a parent or guardian to sign a release form,'' she said sweetly. She was going to kill Vic.

"WRONG, WRONG, WRONG," Phoebe said as she, Victoria, Terri and Angela sat in the bar of a Mexican restaurant sharing a plate of nachos. "You can't possibly go out with a studly guy like Vic Steadman and not sleep with him."

"The sex has just messed up our lives," Angela said. The first day of the Expo was over, and her hands ached.

"It's not getting any that makes you crazy," Terri interjected.

"I was fine before I met Vic," Angela insisted.

"That's because you didn't know what you were missing." Victoria smiled wickedly. "Now that you know…" She shrugged.

Angela took a swig of her diet soda. "I never knew my friends were such a bunch of sex maniacs."

"We're healthy, nonrepressed women," Phoebe said indignantly. "You'll just have to trust us on this. You lust after this guy, right?"

"Well…"

"You do. I saw the way you kissed him. If you hang out with him and don't give yourself an outlet for all that lust, you'll explode."

"I told Vic it was a dumb idea," Angela said glumly. "I guess we just won't see each other—"

"Wait, wait, wait," Phoebe interrupted. "You mean this no-sex thing was *his* idea?"

"Yeah."

"Oh, man. If his number-one priority isn't sex, then he must have it bad for you."

"As in, he's in love," Victoria added.

"If you let this one get away, you deserve to be an old maid."

"Phoebe!" Victoria scolded, putting an arm around Angela. "Old maid is an antiquated term. Not every woman chooses marriage."

"I'm only twenty-six," Angela added. "Plenty of time to find the right guy. Or not. I like being single and independent."

"Oh, come on," Phoebe argued, "you have dreams of a white picket fence. I see it in your eyes. You're never going to reach that goal if you don't put forth a little more effort."

"You know what I think?" Terri said.

"No," Angela said, "but I guess I'll find out, won't I?"

Terri went on, waxing enthusiastic despite Angela's obvious disenchantment with the conversation. "I think you're afraid you'll fail at this relationship thing, so you're getting out before it even has a chance to grow."

"Hey, he's the one who called it off," Angela objected. "And stop psychoanalyzing me."

"He's waffling," Phoebe said. "You owe it to yourself to try one more time. What if he's the one?"

She waved away that suggestion. She didn't believe that each person had a one and only. Yet Vic was the closest she'd ever come to a perfect match. If only he didn't have the same effect on her brain as a shot of Novocain.

"How come Sarah didn't join us?" Angela asked brightly, eager to change the subject. "I thought she was coming to the Expo after her nephew's soccer game.''

''Yeah, me too,'' Terri said. ''I hope everything's okay.''

The other women looked uneasy.

''Why wouldn't it be?'' Angela asked.

''Maybe you've been a little too preoccupied to notice,'' Victoria said, ''but she's having some problems.''

''What kind of problems?'' Not health, Angela hoped fervently.

''The marital kind,'' Phoebe said.

Angela sank back in her chair. She'd had no idea. She'd been so wrapped up in her melodramatic love life she hadn't spared a thought for anyone else, least of all quiet Sarah, who would never think of burdening her friends with her problems. Right now, Angela felt lower than a snake's belly, especially since the others appeared to know all about Sarah's situation. ''Is there anything we can do?'' she asked.

''Just be there for her, I guess,'' Terri said. They all sat in silence for a few moments, lost in thought.

Then Phoebe suddenly brightened. ''So, Angie, are you gonna go along with this no-sex rule of Vic's?''

Angela winced. She thought they'd covered this territory already.

Victoria dismissed the idea of a no-sex relationship with a wave of her hand. ''Like that's gonna last.''

They finished up the nachos, then Angela ducked out while her friends ordered a round of beers. Were they right? Maybe she and Vic hadn't really tried hard enough. And maybe she was afraid, as Terri had said. Breaking off with Vic had hurt. It had hurt a lot. But how much worse would it be if they'd been seriously dating for months or years, and then he'd decided to dump her?

But if she always worried about how a relationship was going to end, she would never date anybody seriously. She would never get married and have the children she wanted someday, because she'd be too worried about the possibility of divorce.

"Time to kick that attitude in the butt," she decided as she let herself into her apartment. She was going to give this thing with Vic another try, under whatever stupid terms he wanted. If she made a fool of herself, if she got hurt again, well, she wouldn't be the first.

She read his phone number from the pad by the phone and dialed it.

Chapter Ten

Vic had just gotten home from the Expo, and he was dog tired. Walking those concrete floors for eight hours straight did terrible things to his body. No wonder Angela had found so many knots when she'd worked him over.

Angela. He'd give over his entire retirement fund to have her sitting in his living room right now. He would give *her* a massage.

Just the thought of her, naked and pliant beneath his hands, made him hard. No woman had ever gotten to him the way she did. What was he going to do about her? He didn't really want to be her enemy, and he'd realized that the moment those hurtful words were out of his mouth. That was why he'd jumped at the slight opening she'd given him.

He'd just settled into his favorite chair with a bowl of popcorn and was perusing the TV schedule, looking for a Stars game, when the phone rang. He almost didn't answer it. He wasn't up to a marathon conversation with his mother. But he happened to glance at the caller ID box, and he spilled his popcorn as he lunged for the phone.

"Hello? Angela?"

Pause. "Yeah. You must have caller ID."

"To screen out the sales calls." He resisted the urge to apologize for leaving her holding the bag that afternoon. *She* was the one who'd jumped into his lap and kissed him in front of God and everyone.

"How's your back?" she asked.

"Still needs work. Maybe I could make an appointment at the clinic."

"I'm sure Daria would be happy to work you over." Daria was a part-time massage therapist who filled in for Angela sometimes when she got too busy.

"I don't want Daria. I want you."

"We've established that."

"Are you busy?"

"Painting my toenails."

"Can I come over?"

"No."

No? Why had she called, then?

She proceeded to explain. "If you came over right now, you'd end up spending the night, we'd get no sleep, I'd probably be late for the Expo tomorrow—"

"It doesn't start till noon. Anyway, I don't have to spend the night. I'll be gone by midnight. Swear on a stack of Bibles."

"No."

Okay. She was the one who'd called him. If he just kept quiet, he'd find out why.

"I'd like to get together next week. We could go

to a movie, or a play, or maybe have dinner. Out. Away from my apartment.''

So she was willing to try his crazy suggestion after all. ''That's great, except I work evenings all next week. Three till eleven.''

''Oh. How about lunch, then? I could take a long lunch on Tuesday.''

Lunch didn't sound like nearly as much fun, but he'd take what he could get. ''You got it. I'll pick you up at the clinic at eleven-thirty, so we can beat the lunch crowd. Then we can go for a walk in the park and feed the ducks.''

''Perfect. I'll see you then.''

After Vic hung up, he felt miraculously better. His back didn't hurt, he wasn't tired anymore. He would see Angela on Tuesday.

Maybe this stupid idea of his would work. He would really get to know Angela. He would learn about her tastes, her history, her family. They would talk about books they'd read. They would see movies, and he'd find out whether she liked those low-humor films that were one of his secret vices.

Inevitably, he would discover some things about Angela he didn't like. The gloss would wear off. He wouldn't think about her night and day anymore. Maybe then they could slide into an easy, no-demands physical relationship.

This could work. It could really work.

ON TUESDAY Angela's last morning client left at eleven o'clock, so she went into the bathroom to primp for her date. She touched up her makeup, twisted her hair into a French braid, lotioned up her arms and put a coat of clear polish on her short nails.

This morning she'd chosen her best uniform, though it was still uninspiring—a turquoise tunic top with a zipper down the front, and matching pants. She lowered the zipper just enough to reveal a tiny bit of her black sports bra. It would have to do.

Sarah came into the bathroom just as Angela was spritzing on perfume. "Uh-oh. Someone's got a date."

"Didn't I mention it?" Angela asked casually.

"No, you didn't, and you know it. Is it Vic?"

"Of course," Angela admitted.

"I heard about that no-sex rule. You don't really expect that to work, do you?"

"It's going to work fine. I'm determined to find out if there's anything to base this relationship on besides the physical. And there's no way to do that when the physical completely overshadows everything else. I mean, that's how you and Dan got together, right? You said you weren't intimate till the wedding night."

As soon as the words were out of her mouth, Angela wanted to bite her tongue off. If Sarah wanted to talk about her marriage, she would bring it up herself.

Sarah snorted. "Big mistake."

"Really?" Angela leaned against the bathroom counter, no longer interested in primping. She used to think Sarah's marriage was paradise on earth. They had a four-month-old baby, and they'd just bought a new house.

Sarah took two aspirin from a bottle in her purse and downed them with a gulp of water from the sink. "Oh, I suppose it would have been okay, if Dan had been serious about celibacy. I thought it was a lifestyle choice we were making together. Turns out I was the only one making that choice."

"No! Dan was cheating?"

"I only found out a little while ago. I had some complications after childbirth, and I couldn't...well, you know, for a long time. Dan moaned and groaned about it, and I said, 'Oh, honey, it's no different from when we were dating. You survived then, and you'll survive now.' And you know what he said?"

Angela shook her head, almost afraid to hear.

"He said, 'Yeah, but that was different. I wasn't completely celibate then.'"

Angela gasped. "What did you say?"

"I flipped out. It seems Dan was getting a little on the side, justifying it because I was denying him, and we weren't married yet."

"That rat!"

"Now he swears he's been faithful since we got married, and I believe him...I think...but knowing he betrayed me with someone else while we were engaged has taken the bloom off the rose, let me tell you."

Angela could only imagine. "Are you going to do anything about it?"

Sarah sighed. "I don't know. We've got a daughter

now. Dan is a good father. I'm in counseling so I can 'learn how to forgive—'''

"Oh, please. Like it's *your* problem, something *you* have to get over, while he's living guilt free." When Angela realized she was sounding a bit strident, she softened. "Sorry."

Sarah smiled. "No, it's nice to have friends who don't tippy-toe around the subject. Anyway, I told you that as a cautionary tale. If Mr. Macho Cop isn't getting it from you, he might be looking elsewhere."

Angela wrinkled her nose. Maybe he would. She and Vic hadn't said a word about exclusivity. He could see someone else if he wanted.

The thought made her blood boil. He'd better not. He'd just better not.

Vic showed up promptly at eleven-thirty, and he brought his motorcycle. "If you'd rather not ride the bike, we can take your car," he said. "My Bronco is getting a tune-up."

"No, we can take the cycle," Angela said. "It'll be easier to find a parking place." Besides, she wanted those few minutes to hold on to him. If they weren't going to bed, she had to take her thrills where she could get them.

She fastened on her helmet and climbed on behind Vic, wrapping her arms securely around his torso. Oh, Lord, he smelled good. She'd forgotten what a turn-on this was, hanging on to Vic for dear life as he masterfully guided the bike through Oak Lawn traffic. By the time he pulled in to a parking place, she was throbbing in places not to be mentioned in polite company. Thank goodness they were in a public place.

They'd stopped at Lucky's Café, a down-home diner with a modern flair. Along with burgers and fries and meat loaf, one could order veggie tacos, spinach quesadillas and beer from the latest trendy microbrewery.

"I love this place," Angela said as they climbed off the bike.

"Me, too. One nice thing about dating a cop—we know where all the good restaurants are."

"And you get free coffee."

Angela ordered her usual, the veggie tacos, while Vic fell victim to the temptation of a cheeseburger. They talked while they waited for their food.

Angela learned the gender, age, location and occupation of all of Vic's siblings, and traded like information. They talked about where they'd gone to school, what pets they'd had growing up, movies, books, getting more deeply into subjects they'd just brushed on during their last date.

As they ate their lunch, they ventured into trickier territory—politics and religion. To her delight, Vic had the same middle-of-the-road attitude she did where politics were concerned. As for religion, she was a sporadic Catholic, he was a lapsed Presbyterian. They both attended church on holidays. Angela's current beliefs leaned toward New Age stuff, and Vic listened with what she thought was genuine interest when she blabbed at length about quantum physics and how it related to astral projection.

"Have you ever actually done that?" Vic asked. "Left your body, I mean."

"No," she said with a shrug and a guilty smile. "I'm not sure I really believe it's possible. But I like to keep an open mind."

"I think I astral project sometimes at night, when I dream," Vic said matter-of-factly. "I fly around the neighborhood, and I see things in incredible detail and remember them, too."

"Wow."

Angela had never met a man who didn't ridicule her somewhat unorthodox beliefs. This was cool.

"Your clinic is kind of New Age-y, too, isn't it?" Vic asked.

"Yeah. We were all working for another health-care facility, which shall remain nameless, and we dreamed up this idea for a clinic that would use the best of Western medicine combined with alternative therapies. The patient takes an active part in deciding his or her own therapy."

"You're part owner, then?"

"Yeah. Dr. Nausbaum owns half. Phoebe, Victoria, Sarah and I own the other half. We're not getting rich yet, but we've only been in business a year. Gosh, listen to me, I'm just blathering."

Vic laughed. "I like seeing you talk about something you're passionate about. Your eyes shine and your face turns pink. It's almost like—" He stopped himself, apparently thinking better of whatever it was he was about to say.

Angela had an idea of what that was. "Don't go there," she cautioned him with an impish smile.

"No, wouldn't dream of it. You ready for some serious duck feeding?"

They got a to-go box for their leftovers, of which there were plenty because they'd both been so busy talking they'd forgotten to eat.

A few minutes later Vic pulled the bike in to the parking area behind the Dallas Theater Center, which backed up to the heavily wooded Turtle Creek. A walking path meandered up and down the creek for several blocks, and there were always ducks and geese hanging out, waiting for a handout.

Angela spotted a group on the opposite bank, so they crossed over on a picturesque wooden bridge. Few other people had chosen to spend their lunch hour here, so except for the occasional jogger passing by, they had the place to themselves.

The ducks went ecstatic when they realized scraps were to be had. Angela and Vic laughed at the way they fought each other for tiny bits of bread and tortilla.

"That little one isn't getting any," Angela said. "You distract the big ones, and I'll lure the little one away from the crowd."

They did their best, but the little duck was too dumb to realize he had a private feast all to himself if he would just pay attention to Angela instead of the thrashing crowd. Every time Angela would throw a scrap his way, another duck was already on it by the time he saw it.

Angela laughed until her stomach hurt.

"Come on, it's not *that* funny," Vic said. "What if the poor little guy starves to death?"

"Somehow I doubt that's going to happen." She didn't know why she found the ducks so funny. She just felt good all over. It was nice to be with Vic. She was learning to relax around him, to just be herself. And he didn't seem to mind.

This is really going to work, she thought giddily.

When the scraps were all gone, they said goodbye to the ducks and walked along the mossy bank of the muddy creek. They caught a glimpse of a shy swan—an escapee from one of the estates that lined the creek upstream, Angela thought. A spectacular black-and-yellow butterfly landed briefly on Angela's arm before realizing she wasn't a flower and moving on.

The whole afternoon seemed magical. But all good things come to an end, and though she didn't have another client until three o'clock, she had other duties.

"You've looked at your watch three times in the last ten minutes," Vic observed.

"I really should be getting back to work," she admitted. "It just seems a shame to clean out filing cabinets on a day like this."

"Are you sure you have to go back?"

"Positive." It was oh-so-tempting to blow off the whole afternoon and just indulge herself in Vic's company. But that was the sort of thinking that would get her in trouble. Moderation was the key here. A little bit of Vic at a time, but not enough to muddle her thinking.

She wasn't sure that was possible.

As they started back the way they came, Angela felt a chill in the air. "Is it my imagination, or is it getting darker?"

In answer to her question, thunder rumbled in the distance.

"There was no mention of rain in the forecast," she said. "I'm sure of it."

"Yeah, but this is Texas," he reminded her. "Storms can come up any time. How do you feel about a wet motorcycle ride?"

"We can probably beat the rain," she said without a lot of conviction. The words had scarcely left her mouth when the first fat drops began to fall through the canopy of leaves above them.

Vic grabbed her hand. "Let's move it."

They started running, but the race was already lost. The skies opened up, and sheets of rain fell all around them and on them. Angela laughed, but the rain was cold and her teeth were chattering. They were still a good ten-minute hike from the bike, which wouldn't afford them any shelter anyway.

"Up there." Vic pointed up above them where the ground rose to meet the backyard of some mansion. Perched on the miniature cliff, surrounded by overgrown vegetation, were the remains of what had once been an open-air pavilion. "Looks like there's still part of a roof. We can take shelter there till it lets up."

They had to climb the rain-slick hill to reach the shelter. Angela lost her footing several times, but Vic was right beside her, catching her by the arm until she regained her balance. He had to practically drag her up the last few feet.

The pavilion was bigger than it had looked from below. A corner of the roof was still intact, affording a sizable dry spot and even an accommodating stone bench.

Vic dusted off the bench with his sleeve. "This isn't so bad. Have a seat."

She did. It was kind of cozy. The rain drove down all around them, lightning flashed, thunder crashed, but their little cocoon was dry and out of the wind.

"You're shivering," Vic said.

"Just a little."

He sat down beside her and put his arm around her. She leaned gratefully into him, absorbing his body warmth. Unfortunately his nearness brought back untimely memories. So far this afternoon she'd managed to keep a leash on her physical attraction for Vic. But sitting this close to him, with his face only inches from hers... All she had to do was turn her face up, and a kiss would be only a breath away.

Did "no sex" mean no kisses? She didn't think so. Kissing and cuddling was a legitimate part of courtship. They weren't saints, after all. Following her instincts, she turned her head to claim that kiss she knew was just waiting for her.

He was apparently waiting for her to do just that. The first touch of their lips was exquisite, the taste of him incredible. It was like a first kiss all over again, the surprise, the discovery, the gradual deepening, her heart fluttering madly.

He pulled her into his lap so he could do a really thorough job of the kiss. Angela lost herself in the wonder of it.

When next she was truly aware, she had unbuttoned his shirt and plastered her hands against his hard, wet chest. He had pulled down the zipper on the front of her uniform and was caressing her breasts through her bra.

There were no crowds of gawkers to stop them. Even without the concealing bubble of rain, the pavilion was protected by vegetation and couldn't be seen from the house it belonged to.

Vic pulled the stretchy sports bra up and over her breasts, baring them to the cool air. He leaned down to kiss first one hard nipple, then the other, while Angela squirmed in mindless pleasure.

"I want you," he said on a groan.

"Unh," she said by way of agreement. Her tongue didn't seem to be attached to her brain anymore.

"I don't have any protection with me."

That got her attention. "We can't—"

"I know." But that didn't slow him down any. The way he managed to peel her out of those wet clothes almost without her notice was truly magic. The way she didn't object was almost criminal. Moments later he had her leaning up against a crumbling stone wall, writhing with pleasure, using nothing more complicated than his talented fingers.

Though she had no idea what she was doing, instinct drove her to bring him pleasure any way she could. Judging from his response, she must have been doing something right.

When they'd exhausted all possibilities that didn't involve a pregnancy risk, Angela cuddled with him on the stone bench. The rain was letting up. Her lust-induced daze was lifting, too.

"You know what?" she asked.

"What?"

"This no-sex rule isn't working."

Chapter Eleven

Angela made it back to work in time for her three-o'clock, but just barely. The rain had stopped as abruptly as it had begun, and Vic had insisted they swing by her apartment so she could change into dry clothes, then he'd dropped her off and headed straight for work. He'd probably been a few minutes late, and Angela wanted to kick herself.

She wasn't sure how much trouble he would get in, if any, but she knew how troubling it was to him not to perform his job perfectly.

Angela herself was the subject of more than a few speculative glances from her co-workers, but fortunately her client was there, so there was no time for questions. Mr. Dickson, a middle-aged man with a severe muscle strain in his back, responded well to her ministrations. She lost herself in the pleasure of bringing relief to someone in pain. But when he left a few minutes later, all smiles, Phoebe and Victoria were on her like those ducks on bread scraps.

Victoria waggled one finger at Angela and clicked her tongue. "You changed clothes."

"I got caught in the rain. I was drenched."

"Uh-huh," Phoebe said. "Let me guess. Your no-sex rule flew right out the window."

How did they know? Angela wondered. Did all of her guilty secrets shine right out of her eyes? "I did not spend my lunch break having sex," she said distinctly. She was telling the truth, so long as she used the White House definition of sex.

"Just part of it," Phoebe said. "Oh, I'm so glad y'all are back together."

"I'm not sure we are." Angela busied herself with her appointment book, hoping her friends would take the hint. No such luck. They were curious as a litter of kittens and twice as annoying.

"So what's the problem this time?" Phoebe asked, sounding a bit exasperated. "You've decided you don't like his earlobes? He eats too much meat? What?"

"His earlobes are fine, and carnivores don't bother me. In fact, he's altogether perfect. Which is why I can't keep my mind off him."

"Or your hands, apparently," Phoebe quipped.

Angela closed her appointment book and leveled a look at her two well-meaning friends. "Don't you all get it? Vic's not the problem. I am. I turn into a different person when I'm around him. Crazy, irresponsible, absentminded—"

"Angie, that's perfectly normal," Phoebe said. "Your problem is, you're fighting it. Why don't you just wallow in it?"

"Yeah," Victoria agreed, shaking her head vigorously. "Remember that guy I fell for last year?"

"Randy the Rut?" Angela frowned in distaste.

"Yeah. Remember how crazy I was? I bought CDs of every song we heard together on the car radio. I learned how to cook Indian food because he said he liked curry. I filled my closet with blue outfits because he said blue was his favorite color. I even dyed my hair red."

Phoebe laughed at the memory. "You were really a basket case."

"And," Angela said, "as I remember, the relationship lasted all of, what, three weeks?"

"Twenty-six days. They were the most glorious twenty-six days of my entire life," Victoria said, whirling around Angela's office like some ingenue heroine in a musical.

"And when you broke up?" Angela asked pointedly.

Victoria sagged. "Oh, it was dreadful. I found out he was a two-timing jerk, and I wanted to die."

"Yeah, exactly," Angela said with a satisfied nod.

Victoria shrugged. "I got over it."

"Oh, Angie," Phoebe said, "there's no law that says Vic's gonna turn out to be a jerk or anything. Have some fun. Go with it. Get Sylvia to prescribe some birth-control pills, for heaven's sake, so you don't have to worry about *that*."

"So you think I should just 'go with the flow' and stop worrying?" Angela asked, toying with the idea. It had more than a little appeal.

"Yeah, don't analyze it so much," Victoria said. "Stop looking for potential problems."

"The problems are real. I was late for work—again."

"I'm late for work at least once a week," Phoebe said, "and it hasn't killed me yet. Besides, in a week or two you'll settle down and you won't be so crazy."

"Yeah, you'll realize your perfect man has feet of clay. That's inevitable."

"Oh, no. I don't think so," Angela said. "Vic is perfect."

Victoria and Phoebe burst into simultaneous peals of laughter.

"Wait till the first time he cuts his toenails in front of you," Phoebe said.

"Or worse," Victoria added, "trims his nose hair."

"He doesn't have nose hair."

This prompted another round of hysterical laughter. Phoebe finally managed to get herself under control. "Oh, Angie, you really are a babe in the woods. You'll have to trust us on this. You're in love with the guy. Enjoy it, you've earned it. Stop worrying about being punctual and about your exercise routine and your sensible diet. Splurge on some new, sexy clothes. Live it up. After a while you'll either start hating the guy, or things will settle down to normal and you'll marry him."

Victoria nodded in agreement.

Marry him? Angela was still reeling from the idea

that she might be falling in love. Marriage wasn't even in the picture.

VIC RODE HIS CYCLE like a bat out of hell, threw on his uniform at the station and slipped into the back of the lecture hall just as Captain Sikes was finishing up the second-watch briefing.

"Well, Corporal Steadman, I see you've decided to make an appearance," Sikes gibed.

"The weather, sir. Flash flooding." Inwardly he winced. He'd never lied to the captain before.

Sikes waved away the excuse. "See me in my office before you leave on patrol." He nodded his dismissal to the rest of the crew.

Bobby Ray sidled up to Vic. "Uh-oh. You're in trouble, Romeo."

"I was five minutes late."

Bobby Ray shrugged. "I'll meet you out at the car."

Vic's lunch felt like cold lead in his stomach as he made his way to the captain's office. This must be how a little kid felt when he got called in to see the principal, he thought, though he didn't know for sure. He'd been a good kid, and he'd never gotten into any serious trouble at school.

He tapped on the open door. "You wanted to see me, Captain?"

"Oh, yeah. Come in." Captain Sikes, a burly, freckle-skinned man with fading red hair cut military short, flipped through his phone messages, leaving

Vic on tenterhooks. Finally he spoke. "That transfer you requested? To the burglary unit?"

Vic suddenly couldn't breathe, but he managed to croak out a "Yes, sir." This was it, then. Sikes was going to tell him to take a flying leap, that he didn't have an ice cube's chance in hell of getting a promotion, or a detective's slot, or anything else unless he shaped up.

"The damn bureaucrats lost your paperwork," Sikes said. "All those stupid forms you have to fill out. I hope you kept a copy of everything."

It took Vic a couple of seconds to realize what the captain had said. "Uh, yes, sir."

"I figured. Get me a copy as soon as possible, and I'll fax everything back to them."

"Yes, sir."

Vic made a quick escape from the office and the building. Bobby Ray was waiting for him at the car.

Bobby Ray didn't even ask what the captain had wanted. He seemed to be much more interested in Vic's love life. "So, did you see her? You were late, so I figure it's her fault."

Vic managed to smile. How could he not, just thinking about their frantic sort-of-lovemaking? He had yet to make love to the poor woman in a proper bed, or with the appropriate attention to detail she deserved. They always seemed to be so crazed, so rushed. "Not her fault. Mine. She's turned me into a sex-obsessed lunatic."

"If you have to be a lunatic, that's the best kind," Bobby observed as they climbed into the car. This time, Vic drove. He was determined to follow every order to the letter from now on.

"I don't exactly enjoy being a lunatic, any variety," Vic said.

"There's an easy solution to this, you know."

Vic couldn't wait to hear this. "What?"

"Move in with her."

Vic wasn't so sure. "Right. I'll just pack up a suitcase and show up on her doorstep. What would that accomplish?"

"You spend every night with her. You fight with her over bathroom space and whose turn it is to wash dishes. You accidentally shrink one of her good sweaters, and she shrieks at you like a fishwife."

It sounded as if Bobby spoke from personal experience.

"What a delightful proposition. No, thanks."

"This'll work, I'm telling you. Pretty soon you can't wait to show up for work just to get away from her. Boom. No more obsession. But you still get to sleep with her every night."

Vic had never shared his space with a woman before. The thought of having to put up with some woman's nylons draped over the shower rod, her diet dinners eating up all his freezer space, her long-winded conversations tying up his phone line, had never appealed to him in the least.

That was before the woman had a name. Angela's nylons would be different. He could learn to eat diet frozen dinners for her. He could install a second phone line. All the extra trouble would be worth it if

he had her in his bed every night, gracing his breakfast table every morning.

"I would never shrink any of Angela's sweaters."
Vic didn't realize he'd spoken aloud until Bobby Ray
burst into hysterical laughter.

"Oh, yeah, that'll solve everything. Just lay in a
good supply of Woolite, and your life with Angela
will be all sweetness and light."

"This is ridiculous. She doesn't want to live with
me."

"How do you know? You haven't asked."

"And I'm not going to. Jeez, I'm crazy, but I'm
not ready to give up my independence for any
woman." Brave, macho words, Vic realized even as
he spoke them. But now that he'd dared to imagine
Angela and himself in cozy cohabitation, he couldn't
get the picture out of his mind.

Still, there was no way she would agree. She had
more sense than that. So he decided he would not
even bring up the subject.

VIC DIDN'T SEE ANGELA for a whole week. She had
a massage therapists' conference to attend in Houston,
and between their erratic work schedules, they
couldn't find any blocks of free time in common.

Or, Vic was forced to admit, Angela was avoiding
him. He'd have been glad to come over to her apartment in the middle of the night, if that was the only
time together they could manage. But she wouldn't
agree to that.

He contented himself with talking to her on the

phone. Sometimes they would talk for an hour at a time, but the sound of her musical voice and her sweet laughter couldn't quite compensate for her absence in the flesh.

The following week, however, he was back to working days, and Angela asked him over Tuesday night for her home-baked lasagna.

All day Tuesday he was a walking jumble of hormones. He couldn't think about anything except his upcoming evening. He zoned out halfway through Captain Sikes's morning briefing, and Bobby Ray had to elbow him to jar him out of his reverie when Sikes asked him a direct question. In the afternoon he spent a couple of hours on the firing range, and his marksmanship was so poor he was humiliated.

"Man," one of the other guys said, shaking his head, "I've seen better shots at a Tijuana beer joint."

Vic flexed his injured hand. It was still a bit stiff from his disagreement with the fence, but he couldn't blame his lack of aim entirely on the injury. "I'm a little rusty, that's all," he said, leveling a testy scowl at the guy. Barry had gone to the police academy with him, and the first time he'd handled a firearm he'd nearly shot off his own foot.

"Hey, I didn't mean anything by it," Barry said, backing off a couple of steps. "Everybody has an off day."

Not Vic. He'd always been able to summon single-minded concentration when it came to target practice. He'd been shooting skeet with his uncles since he was a kid.

Angela strikes again, he thought on his way home. What if his preoccupation with her caused him to lose concentration during a real crisis? Would he be able to focus on his job when lives were at stake?

Ah, hell, it was just one bad day. Tomorrow, he resolved, he would put her out of his mind. Tonight, however, he intended to forget about work and think only of Angela.

He was early, but that wasn't unusual. He was a punctual kind of guy. Arriving late on their first date had been difficult. He'd driven around the block three times because he'd wanted to make her worry about whether he'd show.

Now he didn't want her to worry. She worried too much as it was.

Angela greeted him with a warm smile and an even warmer kiss. There was no hesitation, no reticence. Her lips were pliant beneath his—willing, eager, even.

"This is nice," he murmured against her mouth.

"I missed you this past week."

Vic stopped short of telling her just how much he'd missed her. He had to watch the sentiment. Bobby Ray had warned him not to let her know how besotted he was, or she'd have him whipped. Truth was, he wouldn't mind being whipped all that much. His real concern was that an excess of sentiment would scare her away. She was a skittish creature, changeable as the Texas weather, and he never knew quite what to expect.

Vic broke the kiss, knowing that if he got any more

carried away he'd be dragging her to the bedroom and reliving his favorite fantasy. "Something smells good."

"It's either my perfume, or the lasagna."

"Hmm, well, unless you've taken to wearing oregano perfume, it's the lasagna."

She laughed and took his hand, leading him toward the kitchen. She wore a Mexican cotton shirt with a low scoop neck, showing a hint of mysterious cleavage, and snug jeans. He'd never known a woman who looked so good in jeans.

"Dinner should be ready in about fifteen minutes. You want a beer? Soda? Or I have some Chianti, to fit in with the Italian dinner theme."

"Soda, thanks," he said, sitting.

She let go of him long enough to get his drink from the fridge, but as soon as she'd handed him the can, she sat down and touched him again, this time with a casual, possessive hand to his knee.

"How was work today? Did you go to the shooting range?"

"I'd rather not talk about *that*," he said with a grimace. The ice-cold drink tasted great, but Angela's hand, now on his thigh, did things to him. He didn't think she was even aware of how intimately she touched him.

A couple of weeks ago she wouldn't have been this comfortable with him. He liked the fact that she could relax around him, that she wasn't so nervous. Too bad he couldn't say the same for himself. He was knotted up like a sweater that had been knitted too tightly, and he couldn't wait for Angela to unravel him.

"How was the convention?" he asked. "You haven't told me much about it."

"Three days of learning new techniques and practicing them on each other," she said with a shrug. "My hands got a workout, and the rest of me was so loose they had to pour me onto the plane coming back to Dallas."

"Did you have guys massaging you?" Vic asked with a stab of jealousy.

"Sometimes."

"Mmm."

"I like getting massaged by a guy. Their hands are naturally bigger and stronger."

Suddenly Vic felt like a grizzly defending its territory. "Next time you feel the need for a guy to massage you, the guy better be me." His jealous snit was only half in jest. The thought of another man's hands on her made steam come out his ears.

She waved away his concern. "You don't know how to do a proper massage."

"That sounds like a challenge to me." He stood up and stretched his arms over his head, cracking his knuckles.

"Vic, I was only teasing."

"No, I think we need to settle this question immediately." He gave her a wicked grin and stepped behind her chair.

Angela had pulled the front section of her thick hair off her face with a butterfly clip, leaving the rest hanging loose on her shoulders. He scooped up the heavy, silky mass, secured it all in the clip so he had easy access to her neck, and went to work.

So, she thought he didn't know how to give a good massage? Maybe he wasn't certified in massage therapy, but he'd been rubbing girls' necks since junior high. He'd progressed to backs, feet and other nice, soft parts of the female body as he'd gotten older. More than one woman had claimed his fingers were pure magic.

"Um," Angela said as he worked his thumbs over the delicate column of her neck, "maybe we should postpone this until—"

"You don't like it?" He moved his hands to her shoulders, sliding his fingers beneath the loose, gathered neckline of her blouse. She almost purred. He knew darn well she liked it.

"Oh, no, I like it, it's just—"

"You'd like it better if we were both naked and I slathered you with lotion."

"You're not playing fair."

"This is war, babe. You impugned my massaging skills." His hands slid farther inside her blouse, grazing the tops of her breasts. When he boldly cupped her breasts through her bra, she nipped at his arm with her teeth. He wasn't sure why, but that little bit of playfulness almost sent him over the line from a slow burn to a full-fledged inferno. He withdrew his hands and pulled her to her feet for another kiss, this one heating up the whole kitchen.

"I never knew a week could be such a long time," she said, tugging at his belt buckle.

He was not going to make love to Angela in the kitchen. He'd sworn that next time they'd make it to the bedroom, and he intended to follow through. So he scooped her up and carried her down the hall.

He couldn't help but notice that this time her bedroom was neat as a pin. She'd tidied up for him, which pleased him immensely. That was his last rational thought as clothes flew in every direction.

"Condoms?" he asked.

"I'm on the Pill now," she murmured as she sucked on his earlobe, "though if you'd feel safer—"

"No way." He liked feeling Angela against him without benefit of any physical barrier. "You got on the Pill for me?"

"Who else?"

Then there was no more talking as Vic indulged several of his favorite recent fantasies, managing despite his eagerness to take his time and love her the way she deserved to be loved, discovering her most sensitive spots, even the ones he never expected to find.

When they were both sated, they lay together in a relaxed netherworld of pure satisfaction, half-dozing. Vic might have been content to just fall into a deep, sanguine sleep, except for something tickling his subconscious—something troubling.

Finally he came fully alert and realized what was bothering him. "Angela?"

"Mmm..."

"Dinner?"

She sat up with a startled gasp. "Oh, my heavens!" She jumped out of bed and ran stark naked into the kitchen, where a filmy gray smoke poured from the oven and filled the room with the smell of burned cheese and tomato sauce.

ANGELA POKED AT the leaden brick of lasagna on her plate and sighed. She'd tried to salvage the center part of the casserole she'd slaved over earlier, but even though it wasn't black, it was dry and tough as an old army boot.

She and Vic, dressed now, sat on her minuscule balcony while the apartment aired out.

"This isn't edible, is it?" she asked.

Vic tried to cut his own brick with a knife. "Oh, I don't know." He managed to free a bite-sized hunk and stuff it in his mouth. Then he chewed. And chewed. And chewed.

"You're a good sport," she said, taking a swig of Chianti. At least she hadn't burned that. The garlic bread was nothing but a cinder. "But you're going to crack a molar."

Vic finally swallowed. "Okay, you win. It's not edible. Want to send out for Chinese?"

"I'm not really that hungry anymore."

"Me, neither. Want to go back to bed?" He looked at her expectantly.

"I'm almost afraid to. Every time we make love, some disaster strikes."

"Not every time. Anyway, what could go wrong tonight? I brought my travel alarm."

"No need. I bought a clock radio yesterday."

"Yeah, but what if we have a power outage during the night?"

Angela pursed her lips. "You're right. Better set the travel alarm, too."

"Okay." He smiled, and her troubling thoughts dissipated along with the smoke in her kitchen. Really, what could go wrong?

Vic helped her clear the dishes and dispose of the ruined dinner. When the kitchen was reasonably clean, she blew out the air-freshener candle she'd lit to get rid of the burn smell. As they passed through the living room, she blew out the candle she'd lit there, too.

She left the one in the bedroom burning, though. It gave off a nice vanilla scent and cast the room in a romantic glow.

"Mmm, this is nice," Vic said, drawing her over to the bed.

"Better than burned cheese."

"No, I mean the whole thing is nice. The room, the candle, the bed…you."

"Us. You want to finish that massage you started earlier?"

"Only if you let me rub your bottom."

"You may rub any parts of my anatomy you desire—and I guarantee I didn't tell that to any of my fellow massage therapists."

"Better not have," Vic growled as he tugged her shirt over her head.

She thrilled at the possessive note in his voice. Her heart raced with each stroke of his hand, each featherlight kiss, every murmured intimacy. Within a few short minutes she had climbed to the height of passion once again, and they made love slowly, with excruciatingly minute attention to detail. Angela had never imagined she could feel so thoroughly loved.

As they started to doze off, Angela remembered the candle. She stumbled out of bed on rubbery knees, staggered to her desk and blew out the candle. Vic welcomed her back to bed with drowsy kisses, his arms wrapped possessively around her.

She had no trouble falling asleep this time.

When next she was aware, an acrid smell filled her nose. She'd been dreaming about her ruined lasagna, and for a moment she thought it was just a particularly vivid dream. But then she came fully awake and realized she couldn't breathe. The bedroom was filled with smoke so thick she couldn't see the foot of the bed, an orange glow flickering through the ghostlike layers of dark gray.

"Vic, wake up!" she screamed, shaking him violently. "There's a fire!"

Chapter Twelve

Vic came awake with the sensation of smothering. He immediately began to cough.

"The phone," Angela said. "I've got to call—"

"No time," Vic said, coming fully alert and realizing just how little time they had. They were both coughing, and Vic's eyes started tearing up. The room was hot as a sauna.

He leapt out of bed, pushed the nightstand aside and fumbled with the window lock.

"I've got a fire extinguisher—"

"No time!" He got the window open, despite the fact that the hardware was hot as a match head, but when he turned, Angela had vanished in the thickening smoke.

"Angela!" He stumbled through the suffocating smoke, his bare feet encountering burning embers on the carpet. "Angela, where are you?"

"I'm…here. The fire extinguisher—"

"For God's sake, it's too late for that." He followed the sound of her voice, flailing his arms until he encountered her. He grabbed her arm. "We have to get out now!"

"I've got to get dressed," she said indignantly.

"Like hell you do." He didn't like manhandling her, but he had no choice. Though he was disoriented now, fresh air was coming through the window and he moved toward it. They had not even a second to spare; the oxygen from outside would give the fire renewed life.

Finally he found the window again.

"I'm not going outside...." Angela stopped to cough. "I'm not going outside stark naked!"

He did not have time to argue with a woman who'd obviously lost touch with reality. Did she want to be embarrassed and alive, or clothed and dead? He shook her to get her attention, then grabbed her chin and forced her to look at him.

"Climb through that window before I toss you through," he roared at her.

The sound of her sob tore at his heart, but she climbed through the window as he'd ordered. Vic was right behind her; at the last possible moment he grabbed both sides of the eyelet curtains and yanked them down and through the window after him.

Sirens accompanied their hurried descent of the fire escape. When they reached the bottom, Vic wordlessly handed Angela one of the curtain pieces, which she wasted no time wrapping around herself. It barely covered her, and she would be in trouble if the wind picked up. He wrapped the other curtain around his hips so he wouldn't get arrested.

Though it was the middle of the night, a crowd was already forming across the street to watch the burning apartment building. The fire obviously hadn't been confined to Angela's unit. He was relieved to see quite a few people he recognized as Angela's neighbors, including nosy Mrs. Gibbons of the three dead bolts. Most of them looked as though they'd dressed as hastily as he and Angela. One woman was in a skimpy nightgown, and a man wore only his underwear and a T-shirt.

Angela was quiet now, and Vic could tell she was in shock. He took a moment to pull her close. She didn't resist him, but she didn't seem to welcome the embrace, either.

"Are you okay?" he asked gently. "Are you hurt anywhere?"

"I'm fine," she said woodenly.

"I'm sorry I shook you."

"You should be."

"I was trying to—"

"I know, I know. I was acting crazy." She bit her lip, then added, "I guess I should be thanking you for saving my life."

"You're the one who woke me up, remember?" He kissed the top of her head. "Poor thing, you're shivering. Let's find some clothes." Decisively he walked her over to the gawkers. "Excuse me, does anyone have a robe my girlfriend can borrow?"

"Here, she can use mine," said one woman, who immediately shucked off a pink terry robe and handed it to Angela, patting her sympathetically. Underneath the woman wore a perfectly modest pair of pajamas and appeared in no danger of catching a chill. "Do you need anything else? A drink of water, maybe? My house is right over there."

Angela shook her head.

"No, but thanks." Vic wrapped the robe around Angela. She stuffed her arms into the sleeves with mechanical motions. He tried to help her tie the sash, but she batted his hands away.

"I'm okay," she said.

"Sit down on the grass and wait for me here. I'm going to see if I can help." The sirens were closer, but no fire trucks had arrived.

Vic approached the neighbors "I know I don't look like it right now," he said, "but I'm a police officer. Is anyone hurt?"

One old woman was sitting on the curb, holding her head and coughing. Vic zeroed in on her. "Are you okay, ma'am?"

She looked at him and nodded. "Just…catching my…breath.

"Hey, mister!" A little boy tugged on Vic's curtain, nearly causing an impromptu striptease.

Vic hastily rewrapped himself, smiling reassuringly at the boy, who was about five or six. "Hi."

The boy held up his arm, revealing a cut that was slowly oozing blood. "I cutted myself when I climbed out the window."

"And aren't you brave, you aren't crying or anything," Vic said, checking out the injury. It didn't look serious, just messy. "Where's your family?"

"I don't know."

Just then a frantic woman ran up and grabbed the kid. "Todd, I told you to stay with me. You scared me half to death!"

"He's got a scratch on his arm that needs some attention," Vic told the woman. "Do you think everyone's out of the building?"

"My husband got everyone out on the second floor," she said, dabbing at her son's arm with a tissue. "I think someone cleared out the third floor, too, but I heard they couldn't get an answer out of 3D. The fire is worst in that area."

Angela's apartment. "That's where I was staying," he said. "We got out, but our clothes didn't make it."

Relieved that everyone seemed to have escaped the burning building, Vic herded the stunned residents across the street just as the first fire engine arrived, so the firefighters would have plenty of room to maneuver. He told the first fireman off the truck everything he knew, then met the ambulance as it drove up.

"Lady sitting on the curb is coughing pretty bad," he told the driver, "and a little boy over there has a cut." He pointed to where the boy and his parents were fidgeting with his cut, trying to bandage it with a rag. "No other serious injuries that I've seen."

Next he met the police cruiser that arrived behind the ambulance. A female officer got out and gave Vic a surprised once-over. "Steadman?"

"Hey, Detmyer." He'd known her when he worked a beat in Oak Lawn.

"You were in the fire? Or do you always walk around at night wrapped in a pillowcase?"

"It's a curtain, thank you very much. As far as I know, everyone's out of the building and nobody's badly hurt."

But Patrice Detmyer couldn't stop staring at Vic's attire. "I wish I had a camera!"

"Oh, knock it off."

"Wait till this makes the rounds on the department grapevine."

"I really wish you wouldn't. I'm up for a promotion."

She thumped him on his bare chest. "Lighten up. You're not on duty, so no one's going to hold it against you that you're dressed like a gigolo."

Vic glared at her. "You can take it from here. I have to go find my girlfriend."

As he made his way back to where he'd left Angela, he mulled over the fact that he'd twice in ten minutes referred to Angela as his girlfriend. He liked the sound of that. He wondered if she would.

ANGELA SAT VERY STILL on the grass and watched her apartment building burn. Gradually her senses returned. Her lungs burned from the earlier onslaught of smoke. Her feet stung, too, and she suspected she'd stepped on some burning embers. But she hadn't suffered any serious injuries, for which she was grateful.

She watched Vic now as he took command of the

situation, checking on the injured, asking questions, moving people around. Though he wore only that ridiculous eyelet curtain, his air of command surrounded him like a cloak. Everybody listened to him. Everybody obeyed him as if he wore his uniform and badge.

She realized then that the dangerous, take-charge guy who'd first intrigued her and frightened her really was Vic, or at least some part of him. Because he'd been so kind and gentle lately, she'd started thinking of "Evil Vic" as more of a theatrical character than a real man. But he was real, all right. Not that he was evil, but he was commanding and just a little bit scary.

She rubbed her face. He'd shaken her and screamed at her. She would never have guessed he was capable of that.

Granted, she'd been acting like a ninny, and he'd been forced to do something drastic to get her attention. But the manhandling still had shocked her to her core.

Did she really know this man with whom she'd shared her bed and her body?

The fire trucks arrived and the hoses went to work dousing the flames. From Angela's viewpoint, the worst of the fire was on the third floor, her floor.

Had her smoke alarm gone off? she wondered. She didn't remember hearing it. She hadn't checked the batteries in a long time—another example of her recent absentmindedness.

Then a terrible thought occurred to her, a terrible,

hideous, almost incomprehensible thought. She'd been burning those air-freshener candles. She remembered blowing out the ones in the kitchen and living room, but what about the vanilla one in her bedroom? It had made such a nice warm glow, perfect for lovemaking. She remembered that. But she had no conscious memory of extinguishing the candle afterward.

Oh, my God, had her carelessness burned up an entire apartment building?

Vic suddenly materialized beside her on the grass, wrapped in a blanket. "Hi. You doing okay?"

"No. I'm homeless."

"Not if I have anything to say about it."

"My clothes are burning up."

"You can get more clothes, Angela," he said gently. "People are what's important."

Angela bowed her head, thoroughly shamed. Wrapped up in her personal pity party, she'd completely forgotten about the safety of her neighbors. "Did everyone get out okay?"

"I think so."

"God, I hope so. Mrs. Gibbons? And that other lady on the first floor, Florence something or other?"

"They both got out fine."

"Oh, good."

"We can leave, too, if you want."

"And go where?"

"My house."

She was so tempted. But she would be without a place to live for at least several days, until she found a new apartment. If she moved in with Vic, she might have a hard time convincing herself to move back out.

"Maybe I better call Phoebe. Anyway, how will we get to your house? Neither of us has our car keys."

"I have connections. A buddy of mine said she'd take us where we need to go."

She couldn't decide what to do, so she caved in and let Vic decide for her.

The "buddy" turned out to be a woman police officer. She didn't seem particularly warm toward Vic, though. In fact, she treated him with a certain amount of disdain, so at least Angela didn't have to fight jealousy in addition to fatigue and guilt.

"How will we get into your house without a key?" Angela asked, stifling a yawn. The evening's stresses were catching up with her.

"I have a keyless entry."

"State-of-the-art security, huh?"

"I've gone on too many burglary calls to take any chances."

A few minutes later the officer dropped them off in front of Vic's house, a no-frills brick ranch surrounded by tall trees. Angela wearily mounted the steps to the porch, then allowed Vic to guide her inside. He put her in the shower so she could rinse off the smoke smell, gave her a big T-shirt and tucked her into bed. She roused briefly when he joined her in the bed a few minutes later, but immediately dropped off again.

When next she awoke, the sun was just coming up

and she was alone. She found a note on Vic's pillow. "Coffee's made. Take the day off, and I'll see you around three-thirty."

Take the day off? No, absolutely not. She couldn't do that. She had a full schedule, and she wanted her life to get back to normal as quickly as possible. She jumped out of bed, then couldn't figure out what to do next. She didn't have any clothes, or any way to get to work. If she wanted Phoebe to come get her, she didn't even know where she was. She'd been so shell-shocked last night she hadn't noticed which way their patrol-car taxi had driven.

She found the phone on the bedside table and called Phoebe.

"Angela! Thank God. I heard about the fire on the news this morning, and when I tried to call you your line was disconnected! Are you okay?"

"Yes, I'm fine."

"Where are you?"

"I'm at Vic's house, and he's gone to work. I need you to come get me. And bring me a change of clothes."

"You're not coming in to work today." Phoebe sounded shocked. "Sylvia won't even be there. She's doing some prep work for that Women's Empowerment Rally tomorrow."

"I want to come in," Angela insisted. "I have calls to make, things to take care of, and I'd rather have my base of operations at the clinic."

"Ooh, I get it. You don't want to call your mother and tell her you're staying at your boyfriend's."

"Right."

"Well, you can stay with me if you want. You know that. But why would you want to move into a tiny one-bedroom apartment with a slob girlfriend when you can come home instead to a big, muscle-y stud in your bed every night?"

"I'm not ready for that. This relationship is already moving forward at the speed of light. I have to put on the brakes."

Phoebe sighed elaborately. "Oh, all right. What's his address?"

"I don't know. See? I don't even know where the guy lives. I can't move in with him."

"Who are you trying to convince, me or yourself?"

Angela found some mail with Vic's address. She rattled it off to Phoebe, along with Vic's phone number.

"Be there in an hour," Phoebe said cheerfully before hanging up.

Angela took another shower, thoroughly scrubbing this time to get all the smoke out of her hair. Now that she had a chance to really study the house, she realized it wasn't the unremarkable ranch she'd thought it was last night. The ground floor housed the bedrooms; there seemed to be three. Then one flight *down*, was the kitchen, living room, another bedroom and a huge game room converted from a garage. The house was built into the side of a hill.

"Strange," Angela murmured aloud as she poured herself some coffee, then carefully and deliberately turned off the coffeepot. If Vic's house caught fire, she wasn't going to be the responsible one. She didn't actually snoop, but she peeked out into the overgrown backyard and checked out his CD collection.

When Phoebe arrived, she thrust a pair of carpenter jeans and a blue work shirt into Angela's waiting hands, then made herself at home while Angela changed. Unlike Angela, Phoebe had no qualms about snooping. When Angela came out of the bedroom, relieved to be fully dressed, she found Phoebe going through the refrigerator.

"Phoebe!"

"Hey, if the guy had anything to hide, he wouldn't have left you here alone. He's pretty neat for a bachelor, and he actually has food in the refrigerator. Good roommate material, if you ask me."

"I wasn't asking. Can we please go?"

"Aren't you going to leave him a note?"

"I'll call him when I get to work."

Angela shrugged. "Okay, but notes are more romantic."

"He left me one. It wasn't romantic at all, just kind of bossy."

"Hey, if he's literate at all, that's another plus."

Angela called and left a message at the station for Vic to call her, leaving her work number. But by four o'clock he hadn't called.

She was almost relieved, because what she had to say to him wasn't all that pleasant.

VIC CALLED HIS HOME a couple of times and got no answer. He had an uneasy feeling about that, and as he rode his motorcycle into the carport after his shift, his uneasiness grew.

When he came in through the back door, he called out Angela's name. Just as he feared—no answer.

She was a skittish creature, and he would understand if she didn't want to move in with him, even temporarily. He had reservations about that, too. Things were moving way too fast. But he hadn't expected her to fly the coop quite so quickly. Staying under his roof for a few hours wouldn't have killed her.

He called her at the clinic, but Terri, the receptionist, told him she'd gone for the day.

"Gone where?" he asked.

"I'm not sure," Terri hedged, but he knew she was fibbing. She just didn't want to tell him.

He had a terrible feeling that his Angela, his *girlfriend,* was having second…no, third…no, fourth thoughts about the two of them together. Just because a little black cloud of bad luck seemed to be hanging over their relationship was no reason to get superstitious.

Sex had nothing to do with starting fires.

PHOEBE'S APARTMENT WAS tiny, but it seemed a welcome retreat after the day Angela had had. She flopped down on the sofa and kicked off her borrowed sneakers, which pinched her toes. She and Phoebe were close to the same size bodywise, but Phoebe was a couple of inches shorter, and her feet were a size smaller.

Angela had called all of her relatives and close friends to let them know she was all right. Many of them had heard about the fire and were beside themselves with worry. Angela hadn't realized how many people truly cared about her.

She'd contacted her insurance agent, who had couriered a check for five hundred dollars to cover her immediate needs. Her belongings were insured for ten thousand dollars, and her agent had assured her that if the apartment was totally trashed, she would get the full amount. That would come in handy.

She'd gotten her spare car key from her mother, a replacement card for her American Express, some courtesy checks from her bank. She knew it would be weeks before she really felt whole again, but at least she wasn't panicky anymore.

"We need to order pizza," Phoebe declared. "But first, why don't you call Vic again and let him know where you are?"

"I left him a message earlier." Angela flipped on the TV.

Phoebe just as quickly flipped it off. "Okay, girlfriend, what gives? A woman who's just lost everything she owned in a fire should surely want her big, handsome cop boyfriend around to comfort her. So why are you avoiding Vic?"

"I'm not avoiding him. That's ridiculous."

"Then call him."

"He had all day to call me, and he didn't."

"Maybe he didn't get the message. Did you ever think of that? He'll be worried about you."

Angela knew Phoebe was right. And part of her longed to be in Vic's strong, protective embrace, to cry on his shoulder, to let him take over and make decisions just as he'd done last night. But after seeing the way he'd taken charge with all of the fire victims, she felt a bit intimidated by him.

"He shook me and screamed at me last night," she said.

"He *what?*"

"I was sort of hysterical. I didn't want to leave the apartment even though it was burning up around us, so he did it to save my life, but still…" She rubbed her eyes, remembering how humiliated she'd felt. She also knew that he could have knocked her to the ground if he'd wanted. But he'd only done what was necessary to get her undivided attention.

"Oh," Phoebe said. "That's different. It's hard to picture you hysterical."

"In shock, really. Oh, Phoebe, I don't know about Vic. Every time we're together, something terrible happens."

Phoebe laughed. "Are you suggesting you had sex so hot it burned down your apartment building?"

"No. Something worse. I think…I think I left a candle burning."

"Oh, Angela, surely not. You would never do anything like that."

"The old Angela would have checked three or four times to make sure I'd put it out. But when I'm with Vic…" She shrugged. "I forget everything. I could have killed everybody in the whole building."

"But you didn't." Phoebe sat beside Angela and put an arm around her shoulders. "Accidents happen. Not that I believe for a minute your silly candle burned down a building, but even if it did, don't take it so hard. Everybody is forgetful now and then."

"I can't handle being so irresponsible."

"So, what? You're gonna break up with the guy?"

"I don't know. I need time to think about it. That's why I don't want to talk to him tonight."

"I guess I don't blame—" Phoebe was cut short by a knock on the door. She looked at Angela and whispered, "You think that's him?"

Angela shook her head. "He doesn't know I'm here."

Phoebe went to the door, peered through the peephole, then immediately opened the door. "Sarah?"

Sarah, with a pale face and puffy eyes, her arms wrapped around a baby, stood on the front porch. "Got room for a couple more at the inn?"

Phoebe all but dragged her inside. "There's always room. You come in here and sit down. What happened?"

Sarah sniffed. "Dan's cheating on me. He's been cheating and lying through our whole marriage. I left him."

A lot of hugging and crying followed Sarah's announcement, and when it was all over, Angela somehow ended up holding the baby, four-month-old Hannah, while Phoebe and Sarah went out to Sarah's car to bring in her things.

"Well, now," Angela said to the baby, jiggling her

slightly and earning a big smile. "Aren't you a sweetie?" Angela hadn't spent a lot of time around babies, but she liked them. She planned on having a couple someday. However, as she cuddled this one and inhaled her sweet scent, she could have sworn her womb ached.

She thought about the baby she and Vic could have made through their carelessness. A human being, a separate life-form. Their irresponsibility still irked her. And yet...how wonderful would be to have one of these critters for her very own, one with Vic's blue eyes and black, wavy hair.

Suddenly she realized what she was thinking. She was going nuts. She had to stop cuddling this baby before her hormones overwhelmed her sensible resolve. She laid Hannah's blanket on the sofa and put the baby on it, setting a couple of throw pillows in key positions so Hannah couldn't roll off.

Phoebe and Sarah had just returned and were discussing what pizza to order when a booming knock and a very male, very irritated voice yelled through the front door. "Angela? I know you're in there."

Chapter Thirteen

Phoebe had the nerve to smile knowingly at Angela. "Guess you don't get a reprieve after all."

Angela thought her heart had stopped beating. How had he found her here? So much for her "safe haven."

"I'll get it," she said to a worried-looking Phoebe. Then she walked over to the door and flung it open. The man standing in the doorway looked exceedingly huge and hard and dangerous. Still, Angela tried to hold on to a stern expression. "You don't have to take the building down. What's your problem?"

"My problem is you. I was worried," he said. His hard, defiant gaze softened a bit. "You were in a pretty bad state last night, and today you just disappeared from my house without leaving word where you'd be. What was I supposed to think?"

"I did leave word. I called the station and left a message that I would be at the clinic."

"Yeah, well, I didn't get the message."

"Told ya!" Phoebe piped up from the kitchen,

where she was supposed to be minding her own business.

"I tried calling the clinic, but you weren't there, either," Vic continued. "So I wormed Phoebe's address out of Bobby Ray."

"Well, uh, thank you for being concerned, Vic, but as you can see, I'm perfectly fine. I've got clothes, money, credit cards and a place to stay. I'm sorry I worried you."

Vic studied her, as if he was trying to piece together a particularly taxing mental puzzle.

"I'm ordering pizza," Phoebe trilled from the kitchen. "You want to stay, Vic?"

"He doesn't even like pizza," Angela called over her shoulder.

"Why do I get the feeling I'm not really welcome?" he asked Angela. "What's with the cold shoulder all of a sudden?"

"I don't know what you're talking about." But she did. She was treating him abominably, after he'd taken such good care of her last night. "No, wait, you're right. I'm behaving badly. Let's take a walk."

She told Phoebe and Sarah she would be back in a few, then closed the door behind them. They walked to the swimming pool area, which was quiet except for a lone swimmer doing laps.

She perched uneasily on a lounger and looked up at him. "I think it would be better if we didn't see each other."

Vic pursed his lips and started pacing. Nervous energy radiated from his body. He very nearly hummed with it. "Hmm, now why does this sound so familiar? Oh, yeah. You said the same thing two weeks ago." He paused, then pinned her with a stare. "Do you still think we bring on disasters by making love, or do we have a new reason?"

"The same reason. I don't like the person I become when I'm around you."

Abruptly he grabbed a chair, pulled it close to Angela's and sat down, leaning forward with his elbows on his knees. "Yeah, well, I don't know what kind of person you are normally, but around me you're thoroughly lovable. What's not to like?"

Angela's brain had stopped on the word *lovable*. Was it possible Vic's feelings for her were deeper than she thought? She'd come to terms with the possibility she might be falling in love, but she hadn't seriously believed Vic was facing the same predicament.

Settle down, she commanded herself. He meant lovable like a kitten. He hadn't said "I love you," and that wasn't likely to happen in the foreseeable future. From everything she'd heard, everything her friends told her, guys had to be strong-armed into saying those words.

"Would you still think I was lovable," she said carefully, "if I'd burned down a building?"

For a few moments Vic just stared at her. "What *are* you talking about?"

"I forgot to change the batteries in my smoke alarm, and…and I left a candle burning! I was so caught up in being your love slave that I neglected a safety precaution every ten-year-old child knows. You turn me into a complete nitwit!''

"Now, wait a minute. I distinctly remember your blowing out those candles.''

"What about the one in the bedroom?'' she countered. "The one that gave off such a romantic glow, remember?''

His slow, sexy smile started a slow burn inside Angela. "Oh, yeah, I remember the glow. I would never forget how you look naked in candlelight.''

Angela determinedly stared at a crack in the concrete. She was not going to be drawn into another physical encounter with Vic. Just because all he had to do was look at her and she went off like a Roman candle...

"The point is,'' she said, "I could have killed a dozen or more people.''

"Wait a minute. The smoke alarm was working. I distinctly remember it buzzing. I thought it was the new clock radio until you woke me up all the way. And I remember you blowing out that candle.''

"You're just saying that to make me feel better. You fell asleep before me.''

He squinched his eyes closed, trying to remember. "The candle was in a glass cup. Even if you'd let it burn all night, it couldn't have started a fire.''

"Well, it did. The fire was worst on the third floor right where my apartment is, remember?''

Vic stood up and started pacing. "Okay, okay. Let's just assume, for the moment, that you left a candle burning and it started a fire. That's why you don't want to see me anymore?''

"I want my nice, safe life back.''

"Safe and boring.''

He was right about that. Her life since she'd met Vic had been anything but boring. Exciting, challenging, unpredictable, with highs and lows that made her wonder if she was turning into a manic depressive.

"You've had the same concerns as me," she pointed out. "Remember being three hours late for work? Seems to me you were mourning the loss of safe, dependable Steady Steadman.''

"I can't go backward," he said simply. "With you, yeah, things are a bit hectic. But after you dumped me—''

"I did not dump you! You're the one—''

"After we agreed not to see each other,'' he amended, "I was a basket case. If me and my life are going to be a disorganized mess from here on out, I'd rather muddle through it with you than without you.''

That wasn't the most romantic declaration Angela had ever heard, but it weakened her resolve nonetheless. How did he do this to her? She'd been so positive they'd be better off without each other. But he had a point. During their brief separation, she hadn't magically regained control of her life. "Are you saying we've cursed each other? Forever and ever? We'll never be in control of our lives again?''

"I would never think of you as a curse, Angela. More like a blessing.''

His words made her go all squiggly inside. She

searched his face for any sign that he was teasing, but he seemed utterly sincere.

"I didn't even know I was lonely or unhappy till you came along." He stroked her cheek, and she couldn't make herself shy away from his touch. She needed it too much.

Now he was using the heavy artillery on her. How could she turn him away? To her ultimate humiliation, she felt tears forming in her eyes.

"Look, Angela. I don't want to mislead you. I'm not looking to get married. I'm not into heavy commitments. But you and I have a chemistry—not just physical, but personalitywise, too. We can't just throw that out the window. Why can't we just...be together and not worry about it so much?"

"I'm not sure I can do that, Vic," she said. "I'm a worrier by nature. I have to analyze everything and look for reasons and connections and A follows B follows C. Uncertainty just bugs the hell out of me!"

And that, she realized, was the real crux of the problem. All her adult life she'd had an idealized version of her future in her mind, starting with the paragon of a lover she'd described to her friends at lunch that day, which seemed aeons ago. No wonder she'd remained a virgin so long! What were the chances such a man would come along?

But he had. No matter what trappings he'd been wearing at the time she'd met him, she'd recognized that he was a good match for her.

Problem was, her ideal encompassed more than just the right man. She had a lifestyle in mind, where she shared an orderly life with her ideal mate, starting with a dignified, romantic courtship, a wedding with all the trimmings, a honeymoon in Bermuda, a house with a porch swing, and two children, a boy and a girl.

Okay, maybe her dreams were girlish and unrealistic. Still, she couldn't just glide along with a relationship and take the little bumps with a grain of salt. She'd found the perfect guy, but now she wanted the perfect relationship, or at least one that roughly fit her expectations.

Her time with Vic hadn't met anyone's preconceived notions. It was just one big sprawling jumble of surprises, not all of them pleasant.

"I need time to think."

"That's what women say when they want to break up but they don't want to come out and say it."

"I already came out and said it once," she snapped. "You wouldn't accept it. Now you've convinced me I shouldn't be hasty, so I want time to think. You've gotten a reprieve. Don't push me."

He pulled her out of her chair and into his lap, though she squirmed in protest. "I will not stop pushing. Not until you look me in the eye and say, 'Vic, I adore you, I want your body and I think we should spend as much time as possible together.'"

"You're making me crazy."

He wrapped his arms around her and kissed her neck. "We'll get counseling. We'll read lots and lots of self-help books on how not to be obsessively fixated on your lover."

Angela struggled out of his embrace. "I'm very serious, Vic. I need time to sort this out."

He sighed. "Okay. I'll leave you alone for a few days. Just remember this." He stood up and took both her hands in his. "We are so much alike it's scary. We could be best, best friends and lovers, too. Despite all the crazy things that have happened, we're lucky we found each other. We may never get offered a better deal in life."

Angela was so close to giving in, to saying, *What the hell. I burned down a building, but I don't care about anything when I'm with you, so let's just stay together all the time.* But she held strong. From now on, she wasn't going to make personal decisions, decisions that had a profound effect on her life, without careful consideration. She would lead with her head, not her heart.

She folded her arms and looked resolutely at her bare feet. "I'll think about everything you've said, Vic."

Silence stretched between them. Angela heard only the sound of his breathing. Finally he spoke. "So long, Angela." The mournful tone of his voice almost made her change her mind. Almost. "Call me if you need anything."

He took off, and she watched him lope toward the parking lot with his easy, graceful strides. She continued to watch him as she mounted the stairs to Phoebe's apartment. He climbed on his cycle and set out without a backward glance.

Angela's heart was in her throat. Already she was second-guessing herself.

The pizza delivery guy sprinted up the stairs behind her. "You order some pizza?"

"Um, yes, come in." She opened the door, announced to Phoebe and Sarah that the pizza had arrived, then went to find money to pay for her share.

"Vic's not staying?" Phoebe asked as she dug through her wallet.

"No. I told you, he doesn't like pizza."

"That's un-American," Phoebe said, turning to the refrigerator for a soda. "Break up with him immediately. He's probably a communist."

Angela laughed for Phoebe's sake, and for Sarah. Phoebe was trying to cheer her up, and Sarah had enough problems without sharing the burden of Angela's chaotic love life.

VIC DOZED OFF during the next morning's briefing because he'd lain awake the night before, wondering how Angela was doing, wondering if she thought about him or missed him, trying to figure out how he could get her to realize how right it was for them to be together. Fortunately a fellow officer elbowed him before he started snoring. He didn't think Captain Sikes had noticed his breach of composure.

But as the officers of the third watch were filing out of the briefing room, Captain Sikes motioned to Vic. "Steadman. In my office."

"Oh, hell," Vic muttered under his breath. Maybe

Sikes *had* noticed the catnap. He wasn't in the mood for another lecture.

Vic followed the captain into his office, dread dogging every footstep.

"Close the door," Sikes said.

Uh-oh, Vic thought as he complied with the request. Not a good sign. He sat in the only chair available when Sikes pointed to it.

"I don't want to delay you too much," Sikes said, "but I wanted to let you know before you heard it through the department grapevine. The detective's slot has been filled. Corporal Billings got it. You know Billings, right?"

Vic probably did know him, but right now he couldn't place the name. He was still trying to absorb the terrible news. He wasn't going to be a detective. He had to keep driving his lousy beat with his annoying partner. God knew when another investigator's position would open, and even then, he probably wouldn't get it. Not with the black marks he was accumulating in his file.

"Good man, Billings," Sikes was saying. He blathered on another minute or two, but Vic wasn't listening. He was trying not to throw up. Barfing in the captain's office would probably be another black mark on his record. *Doesn't take bad news well.*

After murmuring something he hoped was appropriate and dignified, Vic managed to escape Sikes's office, but then he had to face Bobby Ray, who immediately wanted to know what was up.

"Good news," Vic said dryly. "I won't be abandoning you for a detective's job after all."

Bobby's face fell. "Aw, hell, you didn't get the transfer?"

"No."

Bobby had the sense not to press further. They rode around in almost total silence, speaking only when necessary. It was a slow day, for which Vic was grateful. He was more than slightly distracted.

He had more sympathy for Angela's position now. If he hadn't screwed up so much lately, he would have that detective's job. His screw-ups were a direct result of his relationship with Angela.

He tried like hell to wish he'd never met her, but that was impossible. Her presence in his life had enriched it in ways he hadn't dreamed possible. He'd glimpsed paradise. But maybe he didn't deserve paradise. Rewards had to be earned.

As Vic drove down a desolate street in south Dallas, he reviewed the night of the fire in his mind, as he'd done dozens of times over the past few days. She'd blown that candle out. He was *sure* of it. At least, he was almost sure.

He should have paid more attention. Angela was right about one thing: she distracted him as much as he distracted her. He wasn't always at his best, his most efficient and practical, when she was around. As a result of his single-minded attention to his love life, he'd probably done irreparable damage to his career.

He was dimly aware of Bobby Ray, sitting beside him, yelling, "Stop! Stop!" just as he ran a red light.

He slammed on the brakes and ended up in the middle of the intersection, accompanied by squealing tires and impatient horns honking. Mortified by the results of his inattention to his job, he drove clear of the traffic, then pulled to the curb.

"You are a real basket case, you know?" Bobby Ray said, a note of sympathy in his voice softening the criticism.

Vic unfastened his seat belt. "You drive. I'd like to make it alive to the end of our shift."

"What about—"

"To hell with the damn orders." What good did it do him to follow every order to the letter, to rack up an impeccable duty record? One car wreck of a relationship with an impossible woman who in all probability was going to dump him, and his career was down the tubes.

By lunch Bobby was fed up with his partner's foul mood, and the needling commenced.

"You're not eating that perfectly good chicken-fried steak," Bobby Ray observed.

Vic pushed his plate away. "Not hungry."

"You're still mooning over her, aren't you?"

"Who? What?"

"Like you don't know who I'm talking about? You're pretending like you're all torn up over not getting the job you wanted, but really it's the babe who's got you down."

Bobby was partly right. Losing the detective's slot would have been easier to take if he had a warm and sympathetic woman to come home to this evening.

Maybe he'd be taking the disappointment better if he had Angela on his side. Aw, hell, he didn't know what he wanted anymore.

"What you need," Bobby said, "is an uncomplicated woman you don't have to think about. An *easy*, uncomplicated woman."

"No, thanks."

"I could lend you one of mine."

"Just what I need, one of your leftovers."

"No, really. There's this waitress, Nancy something. I made her mad so she won't go out with me anymore, but she might go out with you."

"No, thanks," Vic said more forcefully as he paid the check. "Let's go down to the park and bust some truants."

"Man, you *are* feeling mean."

He was, Vic decided. Mean and cranky. He'd meant to give Angela the time she'd asked for, but if she didn't call him pretty soon, he was going to start eating small children for breakfast.

"Well, you just be grumpy all you want," Bobby said as he pulled up to the curb near Van Zandt Park, an almost barren square of grass and scraggly bushes with a few rusty pieces of playground equipment. It was a favorite hangout for kids skipping school. "I'm in a good mood. I actually got my taxes done on time this year."

Vic felt a sudden surge of nausea. "What's the date today?" he asked, though he was afraid he knew the answer.

"April 15."

"Oh, hell."

"I figured you filed your taxes two months ago."

In actuality, he'd managed to fill out the forms last week, but he hadn't yet mailed them. Well, he could do that as soon as he got home, he reasoned, and still not be late. Close call.

A larger-than-normal group huddled on the park's jungle gym, smoking and laughing. Vic stopped by here almost every day, usually to talk to the kids and cultivate a rapport with them, so that maybe they would develop some small degree of trust for law enforcement. Today, however, he decided to make an impression.

A few of the kids scattered when they saw Vic and Bobby approaching, but the older, braver ones brazened it out.

"Morning," Vic said amiably. "Any particular reason you guys aren't in school?"

"I'm sixteen," one of them said quickly, flashing a sly smile. He was maybe fourteen at the outside. "I don't have to go to school no more."

"It's a teacher's training day," another said. "We got the morning off."

"Yeah, right. Come on, we're all going down to the station to call your parents."

They looked at him in shock. "You're kidding, right?" one tough-looking kid said.

Vic nailed him with a riveting stare that made him shrink. "Devon, right?"

"Maybe."

"Isn't this about the third time I've caught you skipping school?"

Devon had started to formulate a reply when the radio hanging from Vic's belt gave a squawk. "Attention all units, a disturbance reported at the State Fair grounds, someone throwing rocks and bottles at a picket line. Any available unit please proceed..."

Vic held up one hand to silence the kids while he listened intently. "Did you get that, Bobby?"

"Got it. You kids are way lucky today. The man was going to nail your hides." He pointed a thumb at Vic. "We better not find you out here again on a school day."

"Oh, yeah," Devon said, catching on to the fact that he wasn't going to jail after all. "Big bad cops talk real tough. You ain't the man. *I'm* the man."

Vic didn't even respond to the kid's sass. He sprinted back to the patrol car, Bobby Ray on his heels. They were only about five minutes from the fairgrounds.

"What kind of picketers?" he asked as Bobby threw the car in gear and peeled away from the curb. Thank God, something to break up the day's monotony. Adrenaline pumped through his veins, pushing out all dismal thoughts. He had a job to do. "Did they say?"

"You were asleep this morning when Sikes told us about it," Bobby said with a grin. "Some male chauvinist group got a permit to picket a meeting on women's empowerment. Sikes called in some extra people just in case, but it didn't look like it was going to be anything big. More of a media photo op than a security problem.''

"Who's throwing bottles? The women or the men?"

Bobby Ray laughed. "Probably the women. You know those feminists."

When they arrived at the fairgrounds, the scene looked much more serious than Vic had anticipated. More people, for one thing. Crowds of what looked like redneck guys and business-suited women were squared off against one another, shouting, shaking signs, while the police attempted to keep the two groups from physically assaulting one another. Vic didn't see anyone throwing anything, but broken glass all over the ground told the story.

"Let's move," Vic said. "And take the damn keys this time."

Chapter Fourteen

A message awaited Angela when she got back from lunch. "Your insurance adjuster," Terri said, handing Angela a pink slip of paper. "Hope it's good news. Oh, and your one o'clock canceled."

Angela just hoped she wouldn't be going to jail. What if the fire department investigators thought she'd set the fire on purpose to collect on the insurance? How would she convince them it was an accident?

She closed and locked her office door, then forced herself to dial the insurance adjuster's number with frozen fingers. "Ingrid Blair, please," she said to the receptionist as she flirted with the idea of fleeing to Geneva or the Bahamas. She wouldn't look good with prison pallor.

"This is Ingrid."

Angela identified herself, embarrassed by how her voice shook.

"Oh, Ms. Capria. The arson investigator has completed his examination of your apartment building.

The fire was due to faulty wiring, so there's no problem. Your claim will be paid in full.''

Angela couldn't even speak. Faulty wiring? She'd never heard such beautiful words in her life. Maybe she really had blown the candle out. At any rate, she hadn't burned down her building. It felt as if a lead barbell had been lifted off her shoulders.

"Ms. Capria? Are you there?"

"Oh, yes. Thank you. Thank you so much!"

"The check will be sent overnight express this afternoon. You should receive it tomorrow at your business address."

"Thank you," Angela said again before hanging up.

Her very first impulse was to call Vic. She'd left him hanging last night. She realized now that she'd been waiting until the arson investigation was concluded before contacting Vic. She'd wanted to be able to let him know one way or another whether his girlfriend was a jailbird.

What the heck. She didn't have a client for two more hours. She called the station and asked for Vic.

"He's out on patrol. You can leave a message."

"I really need to talk to him," she said. "Can't you radio him or something and ask him to call me?"

"Is this an emergency?" the receptionist asked.

Angela was tempted to fib, but she reminded herself she wasn't the kind of person who did that, Vic or no Vic. "Well, no. No emergency."

"Then you'll have to leave a message."

Angela sighed impatiently. Last time she'd left a

message, he hadn't gotten it. "Do you know where he might be?" she wheedled.

The receptionist sighed back even more impatiently than Angela. "He's probably at Fair Park," she snapped. "Everybody else is there. We're a little bit busy here, okay?" She hung up.

Angela supposed she couldn't blame the receptionist for being irritated. Angela had behaved the perfect pest. At least the woman had given her a lead to Vic's whereabouts.

She caught Phoebe coming out of the ladies' room. "What's going on at Fair Park today?"

"Are you kidding? Where've you been, hiding under a rock? It's the Women's Empowerment Rally."

"Oh, right." Earlier she'd wondered why she hadn't seen Sylvia. Now she remembered. The doctor was scheduled to speak at the rally.

"Why?" Phoebe asked.

"When I tried to call Vic, they said he's patrolling at Fair Park. I guess he's doing security or something. I was trying to find him."

Phoebe grinned. "Find him for what?"

"To tell him I'm not an arsonist. And that I'm crazy about him."

Phoebe, never one to miss a hug opportunity, threw her arms around Angela. "That's great!"

"Yeah, well, I need to tell him before I lose my nerve. Want to go with me for moral support?"

Phoebe glanced at her watch. "I wish I could, but

I've got a patient in five minutes. But you go ahead. You don't need me.''

"I think I will.''

ANGELA KNEW SHE WAS acting nutty. Par for the course. She was just going to have to admit that she had a crazy side to her personality, repressed until recently, that was running amok. But she had to see Vic. She couldn't wait even another few hours. He was at a rally populated by hundreds of women, after all. What if he saw that smorgasbord of females and decided there were plenty of fish in the sea, and one Angela Capria wasn't worth the effort?

It wouldn't take long, she decided as she tooled east on Lemmon Avenue toward Fair Park. She wouldn't want to distract him from his duties. She would just find him, tell him she loved him, make him promise to meet her after they both got off work, and leave.

If the word *love* panicked him, well, he would just have to live with a little panic. He was the one who'd goaded her into admitting how perfect they were for one another. He had to expect that her emotions would get involved. If he didn't want to marry her or commit to her in any way, even with a return declaration of love, that was okay. For now.

Lemmon Avenue was clogged with traffic going toward Fair Park. Ads for this rally had been in the paper and on TV for weeks, but since it was on a weekday, Angela couldn't imagine the crowd would be too huge.

As she turned onto Martin Luther King Jr. Boulevard, she saw TV-news minivans. This was really a big deal, then.

A police cruiser pulled through the front gates of Fair Park. Angela sped up, intending to follow it. Vic probably wasn't in the black-and-white, but maybe the officers could help her find him.

When she pulled up to the gate, however, a uniformed security guard stopped her. "Can't let you in, ma'am."

"Why not? I want to go to the rally."

"There's trouble."

Trouble? Angela's heart went into overdrive. Something had gone wrong at the rally, and Vic was probably in there. "What kind of trouble?"

"They're talking riot."

The man's words did nothing to relieve Angela's fears. Trembling with the fear brought on by a hundred different, ugly scenarios in her mind, she backed out of the entrance gate and found a place to park—illegally, but she didn't care about getting a ticket, though she'd never had one in her life. She had to figure out a way to get in those gates, and she'd have a better chance on foot. Or maybe she could get in one of the back gates. Fair Park had several entrances.

Just then she noticed one of the media vans parking on the street half a block from her. People swarmed out of it—cameramen, burly-looking union types dragging cables and sound equipment, and one blond woman with a suit and a good haircut. The on-air talent, of course.

The newspeople approached the gate en masse, and

Angela fell in step among them. She struck up a conversation with a college-age kid lugging a trunk. He was an intern from Southern Methodist University, she discovered. As they talked amiably, she managed to slip through the gates on the coattails of the journalists.

She bid the student goodbye and hurried ahead of the TV crew, following the sound of shouting she could now hear. What if it was an actual riot? Surely if it was really dangerous they wouldn't have let the press inside. Not that she had any business there. But if Vic was in danger...

She just had to see him, stupid or not. She would stay out of the way, she promised. If there were injuries, maybe she could help. She remembered quite a bit from her two years of nurse's training, and the clinic required her to keep up her first-aid certification.

When she came around the corner of the main exhibit hall, the magnitude of the problem hit her square in the face. Or rather, a rotten tomato did. She was so shocked, it took her a moment to even figure out who'd thrown it. A bearded man in a plaid shirt was pointing at her and laughing uproariously, elbowing his buddy in camouflage. They looked like a couple of survivalists.

"Hey, Leroy," Mr. Plaid Shirt said. "We sure showed that one, huh?"

Angela would have showed them what she thought of their assault, if she'd had the leisure of more time. She'd have punched Mr. Plaid Shirt in his ample gut and kicked his hyena-laughing partner in the shins. But she had to find Vic.

She settled for a rude hand gesture before plowing into the fringes of the crowd, looking for blue uniforms.

Finally she found a pair of cops, busily handcuffing some rowdies with plastic riot cuffs. "Excuse me," she said, "do you know if Corporal Vic Steadman is around here anywhere?"

"Don't know him," one cop answered her. "You might ask Lieutenant Gage. He's in charge."

"Where's he?"

"Look for the guy with the red face and the bullhorn."

"Thanks."

Angela struck out again. Broken glass crunched under her crepe-soled shoes, but no one seemed to be throwing bottles or anything worse at the moment. Mostly they seemed to be milling around waving signs, jeering and cursing. One drunk guy tried to manhandle her, but an elbow jab and a sharp heel to his instep solved that problem.

She heard a man yelling through a bullhorn, demanding order. She followed the sound of his voice. When she found him he was standing on the back of a police truck, so she couldn't exactly talk to him.

There were lots of cops around here, though. She'd promised herself she would stay out of the way, but instead she'd wandered right into the center of the activity. Jostled from all directions, she managed to get the attention of another cop. He hadn't seen Vic, either. But the third one she asked pointed in the direction she'd been heading.

"Over there somewhere, I think. Maybe guarding the police line at the south gate."

Oh, she hoped so. That sounded much safer than wading through this unruly mob, where anything could happen.

Just when she thought she was out of the main area of activity, she came across another pocket of pushers and shovers. Profanity and rude epithets turned the air blue, and surprisingly, some of the worst offenders were women.

Then she saw a familiar face. "Sylvia?"

"Angela! What are you doing here?" Sylvia Nausbaum pulled Angela to the fringe of the crowd. "You'll get hurt."

"What about you?"

"Hey, I'm having fun. I love a good riot."

Angela thought the older woman was only half kidding. Her parents had been activists in the sixties, and she'd practically been raised on picket lines and at sit-ins and demonstrations. "I'm looking for my boyfriend. Tall, good-looking cop?"

"Try that way," Sylvia said, pointing toward a parking lot. "The pigs—I mean cops—are trying to keep people out over there."

"Come with me," Angela pleaded.

"No way. I have to stay here and defend our rights. We've been denied the right to peaceful assembly." She grabbed one hapless male passerby by the collar. "You're messing with the Constitution, buster."

"You women were the ones who broke up the picket line!"

The argument was on, so Angela ducked away. She found Bobby Ray in the parking lot. That was a good sign.

The moment he recognized her, striding purposefully toward him, he gaped at her. "Angela, what are you doing here? And what's that in your hair?"

"I need to see Vic. Is he here? Is he all right?"

"He's over there, he's fine, and you two are nuts," Bobby answered, decidedly irritated. "Just get married and put the rest of us out of our misery, okay?"

That sounded good to Angela. She went in the direction Bobby Ray had pointed and finally spotted her quarry, arguing with a group of rowdy-looking men who stood on the opposite side of a yellow police tape. Relief rushed through her. He was fine. All her worrying was for nothing.

"No one's allowed in!" he shouted. "Violence has broken out."

"Yeah, that's why we *want* in," one of the men argued, hoisting his beer. Another reached to break the tape.

"Sir, if you cross this line, I'll have to arrest you." Vic used his don't-mess-with-me voice, sending a little thrill down Angela's spine. Something about that dangerous dude definitely turned her on.

She'd intended to stay well away from the altercation, not wanting to distract Vic from his potentially dangerous job. She lurked behind a car, just observing, when one of the rowdies spotted her.

"Hey, there's one of them feminists."

Vic turned to look. His jaw dropped. "Angela?" He was obviously appalled to see her there, and Angela wanted to sink into the pavement. "You're bleeding!" He started toward her, concern etched into every line of his face.

"No, it's a tomato!" she said. She was about to tell him to carry on with his job and ignore her when she lost the chance. A brick, which seemed to come out of nowhere, whizzed from the crowd and hit Vic squarely on his head. He fell like a bag of wet cement.

"Vic!" Angela screamed. She ran toward him, heedless of the potential danger from the crowd. But suddenly they became a lot less dangerous.

"Uh-oh, now you've done it," someone said. "Assaulted a cop." And the guys ran in all directions, leaving Angela alone with an unconscious Vic.

She did a quick assessment of his injury. His head was bleeding, but not profusely. She was more worried about the fact he was out like a losing prizefighter.

A woman cop, catching sight of the problem, ran over. "What happened?"

"He got hit by a brick."

"Officer down," she said into her radio. "Parking lot on the south side of the Domestic Arts Building." Then she bent down to do her own assessment of her fallen colleague, her face wrinkled with concern. Her name tag identified her as Fernandez. "Who're you?" she asked.

"Friend of his," Angela said. "Girlfriend, actually.

I was just coming out here to say hi. I didn't know there was a riot going on.''

Vic's eyes fluttered open. "Did you say 'girl-friend'?''

"Don't move," Fernandez cautioned.

Vic ignored the directive and grabbed Angela's hand, holding it so tightly she winced. "Say it again. Say you're my girlfriend.'' He had a goofy smile on his face.

"I'm your girlfriend," Angela said hastily. "I'll say anything you want. Just be still.''

"Can you wiggle your feet?" Fernandez asked.

"I can't," he replied. Angela's first, horrible thought was that he was paralyzed—until he went on, "My girlfriend told me to be still.''

"You can move just your feet," Angela said.

"Oh, okay." He wiggled his feet back and forth obligingly.

"That's enough." Fernandez produced a handker-chief from somewhere and held it against his bleeding head. "Are you in pain?''

"Oh, yeah," he said, squeezing Angela's hand even harder. "I think you should kiss it and make it better.''

"That'll be enough out of you, Romeo," Fernan-dez said dryly.

A group of officers came barreling around the cor-ner of the Women's Building, and behind them an ambulance approached, lights flashing, though the si-ren was silent. Apparently "officer down" had been the magic words.

"You stay with me," Vic said to Angela. "Make sure those doctors don't amputate anything important." He was cracking jokes, but Angela could hear the edge in his voice. He was hurting, and he might've been a little bit scared.

"You'll be fine," she said, knowing the paramedics wouldn't allow her to stay with him on the way to the hospital. She would be in the way. "It was just a little tap on the head."

"Felt like more than a tap." He reached up to feel his injury, but Fernandez batted his hand away.

"I got it under control," she said. "Don't go messing with my handiwork." The handkerchief was quickly becoming soaked with Vic's blood.

Angela stifled the urge to sob. She needed to be the strong one now. "I'm sorry," she said. "It's my fault. I shouldn't have come here, but I didn't know…"

"You're not taking the blame for this, too, are you?" he asked.

Well, why shouldn't she?

He reached up and stroked her face. "Why'd you come here, Angela?"

"To tell you I love you." The words just popped out, right there in front of Fernandez, who looked away and pretended not to listen. Angela hadn't planned them. But it was true, and he might as well know it.

His goofy smile came back. "Hey, that works out real nice. 'Cause I love you, too." Then his eyes rolled back in his head and he passed out again.

Chapter Fifteen

"Vic? Vic! You stay with me!"

The paramedics pulled Angela out of the way so they could do their thing. They threw around a lot of medical jargon, most of which Angela understood, though not all. The gist was they were worried he'd fractured his skull.

Angela gave her sobs full rein as she drove like an insane woman to the Baylor Medical Center, trailing behind the ambulance. It would be a cruel twist of fate if Vic died just when they'd discovered and admitted their love for one another. But surely that wouldn't happen. He'd been conscious and mostly making sense. His injury couldn't be too severe, right?

Unfortunately, that wasn't right. Any number of serious conditions could result from a hard blow to the head—broken skulls and necks, brain damage, hemorrhage, edema, infection…the list went on. At that moment, Angela wished she didn't have any medical training.

She called the clinic from the hospital, explaining that she wouldn't be back that afternoon.

"That's horrible!" Terri said. "Don't worry about a thing here. I'll call Daria in to take care of your clients. You just take care of Vic."

Don't worry? Angela thought as she hung up. Right.

She sat alone in the waiting room, asking every few minutes about Vic, but no one seemed to know anything. He might be in X ray; he might be in surgery; he might be getting an MRI. She couldn't get a definitive answer.

She didn't wait alone for long, however. The waiting room soon filled up with cops, all of them somber. Even Bobby Ray looked serious. He came and sat down beside her.

"Hey, Angela."

"Hey, yourself."

"You think he'll be okay?"

"I'm sure he's fine," she said.

"He's my partner, and I let him down. I should have been watching out for him."

"And what, caught the brick in midair? Don't blame yourself, Bobby Ray. I'm the one who distracted him from his job."

"Cops are trained to handle distractions. Even a distraction as pretty as you." His flirting was half-hearted at best.

"Oh, I'm a real glamour girl, all right. Especially with this tomato in my hair." She'd never bothered to wash away the mess, and now it was dried and felt like concrete.

"Seriously," Bobby said, "I think you're good for Vic."

Angela wasn't sure she agreed. "Whether that's true or not, he's stuck with me."

"Glad to hear it. He's been a real bear lately."

As time dragged by, Angela's co-workers appeared one by one to give her moral support, starting with Phoebe. Then Victoria and Sarah showed up, then Terri, and finally even Sylvia made an appearance, covered with mud and smelling like beer.

Victoria jumped out of her chair when she saw their normally ultraprofessional partner looking as if she'd been dragged behind a beer truck.

"What happened?" Phoebe asked.

"It was great. I was on my way to my car when a guy tried to feel me up. I left him writhing in the mud."

"You go, girl," Sarah said. "A woman needs a man like a fish needs a bicycle." She'd borrowed the saying from a poster in Sylvia's office.

Suddenly all of the male cops' eyes were on the group of women.

"Oops," Sarah said. "Guess that's not always a popular sentiment."

"Men are an inordinate amount of trouble," Angela said, making sure the cops heard her. "But life would really be boring without them."

Her friends agreed with a chorus of "You said it" and "Amen." She even got a grudging smile from some of the cops, warding off the tension. The discussion might have continued, but a nurse entered the waiting room.

"Is somebody here named Angela?"

Angela jumped out of her chair as if she'd been spring-loaded. "Right here."

"Would you come with me, please?"

"He's okay, isn't he?" Angela demanded as she followed along behind the nurse, her heart pounding.

"He's okay," the nurse confirmed, leading Angela into a treatment room. "He's been asking for you."

He was lying on a gurney, naked to the waist, his head swathed in enough bandages to clothe an entire mummy. An IV was attached to his arm, and he was paler than she'd ever seen him, but his eyes were open and he looked at her as if all his senses were functioning again.

"Oh, poor Vic," Angela couldn't help saying. She stood frozen at the door, horrified to see him so hurt.

"I'll take all the pity I can get if you'll come over here where I can see you better," he said. "My eyesight's still a little blurry, but they said it would clear up in a few hours."

She went to the side of his gurney and took the hand he held out to her. The nurse left. "Are you okay?"

"Just a concussion. No fracture. They want to keep me overnight."

"You do whatever they tell you to do," she said sternly. "Whatever it takes to get well."

Vic chuckled.

"What?"

"I guess I'm about as far from your fantasy man now as I could get. I couldn't do dark and dangerous right now on a bet. Pale, weak, vulnerable and needy—that's me."

"No, Vic," she said. "You're the strongest man I've ever known. I couldn't love a weak, needy man."

"What about pale?"

"Pale I can live with, but only till we get your blood volume back up to where it's supposed to be."

Suddenly he became very serious. "So I didn't hallucinate it? You said you loved me?"

"I drove all the way over to Fair Park just to tell you that," she said. "Turns out it wasn't one of my more brilliant moves."

"Chalk another episode up to the Vic and Angela Love Curse."

Angela laughed. "Well, I'd rather be cursed and in love with you than uncursed and living a normal life," she said. "That's what I decided after brooding all day today. I'm sorry I was so hateful last night at Phoebe's apartment."

"You weren't hateful. You'd been through a lot. You were entitled to go a little schizoid. But I gotta tell you, if you'd left me dangling for very long, I was coming after you. I'm not that easy to get rid of."

"Neither am I, and that's a promise," she said, her eyes burning with tears—good tears this time. "I know exactly the kind of man I need, and now that I've found him, I'm keeping him."

"Forever?"

"For..." Angela suddenly lost her voice. Was he saying what she thought he was saying?

"Yes, Angela, I'm asking you to marry me. You weren't the only one who wasn't in top form at Phoebe's apartment. All that stuff I said about no marriage and no commitments—just the lunatic ramblings of a guy trying to hold on to the last vestiges of his bachelorhood. Ten minutes after I left, I knew I'd said the wrong thing. I was already committed to you. If you're not ready for the 'until death do us part' thing yet—"

"No. I mean yes, I'm ready. I love you, Vic, and I want us to be together. Always." She leaned over and kissed him lightly, but when he tried to deepen the kiss she pulled away. "Careful. All your blood will pool in your loins, and you don't have that much to spare."

"I'll risk it." With his free arm he snagged her behind the neck and pulled her to him for another kiss. Off balance, she fell against the gurney, which rolled two feet and nearly knocked the IV stand over.

She and Vic looked at each other. "How fast can you plan a wedding?" he asked.

"Maybe we'd better elope. We might not survive a long engagement."

The treatment-room door opened, and Angela jumped away from the gurney like a guilty teenager. A fiftyish police officer with graying red hair entered, grim faced. Angela didn't recognize him, but she could tell by all the brass on his uniform that he was someone important.

"Captain Sikes. Sir," Vic said. He didn't sound terribly pleased to see his superior.

"Steadman." The captain glanced over at Angela, then back at Vic. "Is this the young lady who's been claiming so much of your...attention lately?"

He didn't even try to sidestep the question. "Yes, sir. Angela Capria, this is Captain Danny Sikes."

Angela nodded and smiled. "Nice to meet you." Vic had said the captain was a tough old boot, former army guy, but he obviously held a grudging respect for his boss. As for Angela, she wasn't sure why, but she liked the captain on sight. Maybe it was the undeniable concern on his face as he looked at one of his troops, wounded.

"You look like hell, Steadman."

"Yes, sir."

"You keep making these trips to the emergency room, and the city's gonna raise our health insurance rates."

"I'll try not to do it anymore, sir."

"That was a joke, Steadman. Don't you know you're supposed to laugh at your boss's jokes?"

"Sorry, sir." He managed an anemic smile.

Angela could only look on in amusement. Vic had said he was a "by the book" kind of guy. Bobby Ray had said something about Vic being all spit and polish on the job. Neither of them had been exaggerating. Vic obviously took his duty and his respect for a superior very seriously.

That fact only made her admiration for him grow.

"Seriously, son, are you all right?"

"I think so, Captain. Just a concussion. I'll be back at work in a day or two, no problem."

"Take whatever time you need."

"I won't need much."

"Oh, stop being such a martyr," Sikes groused, sounding a bit put out.

"It's just that…" Vic started, then stopped himself, apparently thinking better of whatever he was about to say.

"Are you thinking that if you take more sick leave, you'll get another black mark on your record?" Sikes asked. "Is that what you're worried about?"

"Shouldn't I be? I haven't exactly distinguished myself as a model police officer lately."

Angela's heart ached for him. Being the best at whatever he did was important to Vic. She also felt a surge of guilt, even though she thought she'd sworn off the stuff. All those reprimands were connected to her one way or another.

"Is that what you think?" Sikes asked, incredulous. "That you're now the department screw-up?"

Vic said nothing.

"Let me ask you something, Steadman. How many years have you worked for the department?"

"Eight, sir."

"And during those eight years, how many times have you taken sick leave, or injury leave, or time off for a personal crisis?"

"Twice. Counting this time."

"Right. Twice in eight years. Maybe they both happened in a short time span, but everybody goes through these periods when they're a little off center. Nobody's taking notes. Nobody's pulling the gold stars off your personnel record because you overslept one day among thousands."

Vic looked relieved. Angela smiled at him.

"Fact is—and I wouldn't normally tell you this, because I don't like my men and women to get fat heads. But the fact is, you're one of my top officers. Why do you think I stuck you with Bobby Ray?"

"Because you hate me?" Vic ventured.

"Because you're about the only one I'd trust to keep a hothead like him in line, put a little seasoning on him."

"Thank you, sir." Vic's color was coming back.

"Anyway, I just came to check if you were okay. But I can see you're being well taken care of." Sikes winked at Angela. She felt her face flushing.

"Oh, and one other thing. Two other things, actually. Billings didn't take that job in the burglary unit. Seems he was interviewing elsewhere, and he got hired by Houston. So as soon as your doctor gives you a clean bill of health, you can report downtown. In plain clothes."

Vic just stared. The captain had rendered him speechless.

"And I brought something for you." Sikes reached into his shirt pocket, pulled out something that flashed gold and slapped it into Vic's hand. "Wear it in good health.'' He strode out of the room before Vic could say anything.

''What is it?'' Angela asked.

Vic opened his hand and stared at the shiny gold badge. ''It's a sergeant's badge.'' Then he whooped loud enough to bring two panicked nurses and a doctor scurrying into the room.

Angela had a lump in her throat the size of a walnut as Vic assured them he was okay and apologized for scaring them, then showed off his new badge. He'd achieved two cherished goals in one fell swoop. His proud smile was like a balm to her battered soul. She'd never seen him so happy, despite the bandage on his head and the needle in his arm.

''You think maybe the curse is lifted?'' she asked tentatively when they were alone again. She brushed a strand of hair off his forehead.

''What curse?'' he asked with a lazy smile, then took her hand and kissed her palm. ''I told you before, I'm blessed.''

At that moment Angela felt blessed, too. The luckiest woman on earth.

Epilogue

"Well, you survived the engagement," Phoebe said, taking another swig of champagne at the Capria-Steadman wedding reception.

Angela, taking a break from dancing with every uncle and male cousin to the big band orchestra her parents had hired, nodded in agreement. "Amazing, isn't it? Ever since Vic and I became engaged, no catastrophes, not even a small one."

She had taken Vic home from the hospital the day after his unfortunate meeting with a brick, and of course she'd hung around to fuss over him and make him get the bed rest his doctor had mandated. By the next day he'd been feeling well enough to get around, but Angela had somehow never managed to find her own place to live. It seemed silly to move when their May wedding was only a month away.

Angela had wanted to elope, but her mother and sister wouldn't dream of it. "Italian girls don't elope unless they're pregnant," her mother had said. So Angela had compromised and set the date for one month away. Vic hadn't cared, so long as she spent every night with him. He hadn't wanted to let her out of his sight.

"Vic seems to be having fun," Phoebe commented.

"Fun" was an understatement. Angela hadn't realized how much her steady, reliable, usually sober man enjoyed dancing. He was running her family ragged on the dance floor, but the Capria family did love to shake a leg, so he only endeared himself to them. "He's danced with every female member of my family except Grandma Murino, and he'll get to her before long, never mind the wheelchair."

"Has he asked Sarah to dance? Maybe she'd like that."

Angela searched the church hall for her friend, but didn't see her anywhere. "I doubt she's in the mood." Sarah's predicament was the only sad thing in Angela's life right now. Despite her husband's promises that he would reform, Sarah was going through with the divorce. She'd had enough of his empty promises.

Sarah, always a bit on the shy side, hardly said a word these days.

"She's over by the cake," Phoebe said.

"I hope she eats something. She's looking too thin these days. Who's that guy she's talking to?" The man in question had his back to her, and Angela couldn't quite see his face. He wore formal policeman's blues, but that didn't help much. At least a dozen of Vic's co-workers had shown up in their dress uniforms.

Then the man turned to say something to a passerby.

"Oh, my God."

"Oh, my God," Phoebe said at the same time. "I'll kill him. That's all poor Sarah needs is to have my obnoxious cousin coming on to her."

Phoebe started to get up, but Angela halted her. "Wait. Look at her. She's smiling!"

Phoebe gasped. "You're right. She's laughing. I haven't heard her laugh in months."

"Maybe Bobby Ray is just what she needs right now, someone who won't get serious, someone fun and uncomplicated."

"She's so vulnerable, though."

Angela watched the two interact for a few more moments. Chemistry. Definite chemistry. "Sarah's a big girl. She can take care of herself. But just to be on the safe side, tell Bobby Ray we'll turn him into a soprano if he hurts her."

"Who are you two plotting against now?" Vic had come up behind Angela at the tail end of the conversation. He leaned down to nuzzle her neck. "Mmm," he said, just loud enough for her to hear, "when can we blow this Popsicle stand?"

"Not for hours," she answered. "Italian weddings go on forever."

"In that case, want to dance? They're playing our song."

The band had just struck up a slow instrumental Angela didn't even recognize. "This isn't our song."

"It could be. It's slow, and I'm not slow dancing with anybody but you."

Angela's heart warmed. He could be a romantic cuss when he wanted to be. She stood up, though she left her toe-pinching high heels under the table, and drifted onto the dance floor with her new husband, her arms wrapped around his neck.

"Well, maybe we could leave a little bit early," she said. "This rowdy bunch is having such a good time, I'm not sure anyone would notice if we slipped out."

It was true, Vic thought. Police officers knew how to party, and so did Angela's family. Even his normally staid mother had loosened up. In fact, she was dancing with Captain Sikes. Weird.

Vic had loosened up himself. Not just tonight, but all the time. He loved his new job and he was anxious to do well, but he didn't obsess over his performance the way he used to. He'd come to realize what was really his top priority. If he lost the job tomorrow, he knew he would survive with his beautiful, sensible, sometimes crazy Angela by his side.

She leaned in closer. "This is the happiest day of my life, you know."

"Mine, too, darlin'. Mine, too."

*Look for Kara Lennox's next
Harlequin American Romance novel,
TWIN EXPECTATIONS, this December.*

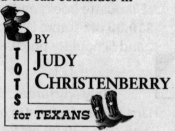

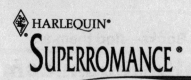

HARLEQUIN®
SUPERROMANCE®

You are now entering

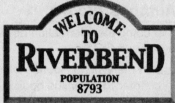

WELCOME TO **RIVERBEND**

POPULATION 8793

Riverbend...the kind of place where everyone knows your name—and your business. Riverbend...home of the River Rats—a group of small-town sons and daughters who've been friends since high school.

The Rats are all grown up now. Living their lives and learning that some days are good and some days aren't—and that you can get through anything as long as you have your friends.

Starting in July 2000, Harlequin Superromance brings you Riverbend—six books about the River Rats and the Midwest town they live in.